Marco Island Writers' Inc.
Short Stories, Poems & Essays
Vol. VI

Marco Island Writers' Inc. Short Stories,
Poems & Essays
Vol. VI
Lead Editor: Jennie Weckelman
Editorial Board:
Jennie Weckelman
Dr. Michael Meguid
Melody Highman
Richard Goldhaber

Layout and Design: Joanne Simon Tailele
Shuttertock cover image # 1950087262
Shutterstock Wreath on Memorial Page #772784482
Publisher: Simon Publishing LLC

Marco Island Writers' Inc.
Short Stories, Poems & Essays
Vol. VI

TABLE OF CONTENTS

SHORT STORIES
&
ESSAYS

What's the difference, you might ask? Briefly, short stories are most often, but not always fiction, while essays are more often non-fiction written through the author's point of view.

To illustrate my point, once, many years ago, my nephew's grade school teacher asked the class to write a story about their fathers. Nephew wrote a fantastical yarn about his father's many accomplishments and outer-space travel. Clearly, it was fictional, but she had wanted an accurate accounting and should have asked the class for an essay.

Short stories are fun to invent and write. No laboring for months, or even years. Write when inspiration strikes! Essays are also fun to write, as well as a chance to explore every-day events, philosophical view-points and whimsy. Both offer the reader entertainment with minimal commitment. We hope you enjoy reading our stories and essays.

Jennie Schwartz Weckelman
Lead Editor, Marco Island Writers, Inc.

The Stylist

Melody Highman

Chapter 1 – Vivian's Grey Matter

Gazing out at the November drizzle, I swipe a thumb over my tongue and rub a smudge from the window. The frenzied squeaking stops once I catch a glimpse of Vivian, my next client. She ducks her head against The Channel's charging winds as she jostles along, ever mindful of the wet cobble underfoot. The wind pulls her backward again. Her damp hair spirals and twists. She tosses her head, swats at her wet locks and bobs left and right, desperate to clear the hair from her eyes.

The thought occurs to me . . . the average weight of a human head is heavier than one might think.

Cradled in my hands, the dead weight of a wet, adult head – a woman with thick, porous shoulder-length hair like Vivian's – even more so.

She's ten minutes early. Punctual as always.

"Hello love!" she sings, stepping over the awkward raised threshold of my narrow Victorian shop. Grabbing the knob with both hands, she heaves the heavy wooden door closed behind her. The paint on the door is thick and uneven. It was the first thing

I'd done to the premises – painted over the muddy grey; swirling blue and a dollop of red in the bucket, adding a dash of yellow and finally just a smidge of black, until the color felt like a reflection of my own chameleon skin.

The shop sign, "Em's", rattles in the wake of the door's closing. The shop is mine. All mine, even if it is only a haphazardly renovated working-class terrace house. To call the décor Bohemian would sound like it was planned that way. It wasn't. Nearby, abandoned factories shadow the landscape. Not a posh place. My customers don't mind – they don't come for that.

I help her slip out of her coat and give it a shake, turning away from the pungent smell of damp camel hair before hooking it over the coat tree. Then a whiff of lilac fills the air. Vivian.

"Forget your brolly, did ya?" I say, knowing it's unlike her. "One can never count on English weather."

"Oh, Mum's got me in a tizz again."

"Ahh, Mum again . . . " I say nodding as we stroll to the back of the shop.

She wiggles onto the padded chair, presses her back deep into the cushion, and sighs. The floor creaks, like always. I've had workmen look at it more than once, but they don't seem to be able to work out a permanent fix. I pump the foot pedal. As Viv stretches her neck back, I gently lift her weighty, silvery mane, slipping it over the sink.

She'll feel better soon.

Her boggy head slips below the water spout. Greyish bubbles swirl down the drain. The thing is her hair color is natural – a radiant silver grey. The same color I've witnessed swirling down the drain for years. Yet now the drain water is clouded. Dirty.

She yields to the manipulation of my willowy fingers as I massage the undulations of her scalp. Cradling her head in my ample palms, increasing the pressure on her skull as I close my eyes and drop my head back, I visualize the spongy grey matter of Viv's brain. The padded tip of each finger explores its topography, the fissured convolutions, the shallow serpentine crests.

Once a client submits, her neck elastic like a rubber band, I keep a keen watch for the moment her eyes slide back in their sockets . . . when the face softens and breathing slows, feet flopping sideways, dangling off the metal footrest.

That's the moment when I know it's about to happen – when

the crackle zaps my chest. Somehow, a conduit forms. The client's energy melds with mine. It's like a violent hum really. A lightning bolt blasts its way through my body, energizing the tips of my fingers and shooting through the bottoms of my feet. The crown of my head pulses as I slide out of my white rubber mules, better grounding myself to the earth.

I do get a rush from it all. The sensation that starts as a snap in the center of my chest, settles low in my pelvis – a thousand needles prickling the fleshy folds. The first jolt hurts. A little. Just briefly. Then there's an explosion of pleasure. Of course, I recognize the elements of addiction. I crave it sometimes at night when I can't sleep. Tossing in my empty bed like a soul at odds with the world.

Like the soul that I am.

Chapter 2 - The Energy

The energy comes in waves. At times I feel like I'll implode from the sheer force of it all. A gift? A curse? I'm not entirely sure. I didn't always have this ability. People certainly thought me odd as a child; I suspect that was likely due to the fact I was the tallest child in the entire schoolyard. Actually, taller than any of the teachers as well.

The energy . . . the capacities . . . came out of nowhere really, right after I opened the shop. Some days it's stronger than others. I can't seem to work out a pattern.

Here's the one thing I do know: I need to direct it. Control it. Use it for good.

After all, once the client is in my chair, they are quite vulnerable. At my mercy. Aren't they?

The responses triggered in my clients seem to hover on the fragile border between pleasure and pain as well. The noises erupting from their bodies are primal. Instinctual moans that escape without their awareness. Groans too deep to be expressed with words. Normal words anyway. Utterances that are barely human. Yet they are familiar to me.

During Vivian's last appointment, I had suggested a short trendy style, to get her back into the salon as frequently as possible - to better monitor her condition. Told her to think about it. Years ago when she first walked into my shop, just after it opened, her hair draped to the middle of her back. A tousle of jagged, frayed strands.

"Something simple," she had instructed me. "Something carefree. Whatever you like." Waving off the comments with a toss of her hand.

"Classic flip girl. That's what you are," I had said, fluffing her hair, coiling the ends upward.

Vivian has worn that simple style ever since. Today she's given me permission to switch it up. "Nothing complicated," she reminds me. "Remember I'm taking care of Mum now. I trust you."

I nod. I know what she means. Whilst she will never say the words, life has gotten more difficult, her Mum now mostly bedridden. Early on, Vivian's mother, Margaret, was a client. One of the originals; when the salon first opened and I was struggling to make ends meet, pay the bills.

Margaret used to work at the butcher counter, round the corner. She'd barge into my shop on her break, frantically untying the double wrapped cord about her thick waist, her white apron splattered with blood, "You won't make me late, will you?"

"I'm ready. No worries." The sharp blade gleamed on the steel tray next to the chair, perfect for a boyish razor cut. She had requested I use the electric trimmer instead. Keep the cut tight, close. Follow the curve of her head.

"You know I can't be late," she'd said, chin up, her posture rigid, her fists in tight balls.

I nodded, motioning her to the styling chair. No time for a shampoo, just a wet-down. Then something strange happened. When I picked up the razor to clean up the back of her neck, it came over me. I clutched the razor hard, paralyzed for a moment. Like I was no longer in control.

"Well, go on then," Margaret had said, her tone tense. I had blinked my eyes, angled the razor, leaned in, and couldn't help but notice the sweat beads mounting on her forehead. Exhaling, I went to work, scraping the razor across the base of her neck.

Margaret's vixen energy was impenetrable in those days. Harsh words spat from her mouth, belittling everyone, everything. I had pressed my thumbs forcefully into her scalp, trying to reach deep into her dark matter. Envisioning blasting the tentacles of anger and fear that had suctioned themselves on, set up base camp in her amygdala.

I sensed the power of her will, her resistance. It was a bit like a tug o' war. In the end, I'd worked out Margaret didn't want help really – didn't perceive the need to change a thing. She'd identified with the feeling of power the vitriol gave her. Proud even. I couldn't overcome it. Not back then anyway. She seemed unreachable. Margaret stopped coming to the shop after that appointment.

Viv had apologized for her saying, "I think Mother finds you rather unnerving. Silly, isn't it?"

I had nodded. I wonder if today, wrapped in sterile sheets, that bull-necked woman still has the stamina to fuel her negative energy. I turn my attention back to the moment. Back to Vivian.

Chapter 3 - Darkness

Mostly good news . . . slightly smaller in size. It's shrinking. Still, I'd expected it to be entirely gone by now. When I first discovered it, it was about the size of my thumbnail. A tumor. Resting on top of the lining of Vivian's brain. She doesn't know. I considered telling her, then thought better of it. That would only create alarm, stress. Possibly feed its growth. She wouldn't even know it was there otherwise.

Sometimes it's good to stay in the dark about things we can't control.

And how would I make her aware of it without raising suspicion? Questioning my sanity? My motives? Risk sending her racing to the overwhelmed health care system? An industry increasingly inundated with conflicting data, spawned at dizzying velocity by the latest state-of-the-art tech. Information they're frantic to decode. It must be like translating hieroglyphics every year or two.

Yeah, I know my place. I'm a stylist, not a brain surgeon. Yet somehow I know this . . . this thing . . . has been invading her. Coursing through her blood vessels. Sending conflicting messages to her organs and extremities.

Viv's hands rest palm down on her lap. I knit them together in prayer position. I move her feet to the center, toes touching in order to connect the right and left sides of her brain. It's working. I stand at the ready, a paper funnel of chilled water in my hand. When she rouses from her altered state, I'll offer the water, wrap a towel around her neck and then guide her from the washbasin to the styling station. She'll say something like, "Sorry, I've lost track of what I was about to say, love." At least that's what she mumbled last time. No awareness that she'd been adrift for almost nine minutes.

After she comes to, I escort her to the styling chair and work quickly, sliding the comb, then scissoring my fingers down the damp strands. Lopping the thick chunks into croppy layers, all the while visualizing Vivian's updated look. Something that will draw attention to her clear blue eyes, her wide, heart-shaped smile. A cut that in earlier days would have matched the fiery nickname of Viv's youth, Dazz – short for Dazzler.

A Polaroid fell from her purse once, exposing the teenage version of Viv, decked out in an A-Line metallic micro-mini, bold Twiggy lashes, and gigantic brassy hoop earrings. Vivian snatched up the photo, flushed red, and stuffed it back in her purse. "Once upon a time . . . " she had sighed.

Yet Vivian still glints of that aura. A stunner really.

I spin the chair and angle the hand mirror downward, gaining a better view of the layered cut, the soft line at the base of her long neck. She squeals. I spin her back. My eyes meet hers in the mock Elizabethan wall mirror. Her eyes glitter. Flashes of white light bounce about her body.

Towering over her, as I lean forward, pulling the ends of her hair, checking for evenness, a lock of my own wavy raven hair falls over her shoulder. She tugs it like a bell ringer.

"Feels like I'm ten years younger!" she chirps.

"You look it too." I smile with closed lips. The right corner of my mouth rises knowingly.

I sweep the vinyl cape away from her body. She collects her purse and earrings and prances to the counter. I grab a pen and the appointment book. "Hmm," she stalls, tapping a finger to her chin, "too much up in the air right now. I'll give you a ring."

I nod reluctantly. Surely she'll ring me and set something up soon, but I'm torn. I sense I won't see her as soon as I need to. I try to shake off the feeling and twitch my shoulders.

Viv's a generous tipper. I thank her, trailing as she heads out. I like to close the door behind my clients to spare them the trouble of lugging the bloody thing themselves. It's tricky and I've got it down pat. After I close up, I immediately sense I'm being watched, a flash of darkness at the front of the shop catches the corner of my eye. A man. Gunmetal eyes peer at me through the shop window. Startled, I shake my head. I don't do men. Only women. Sometimes that causes confusion.

I hold up a finger – wanting to explain, but it's too late, he's on his way. I spin back to the door and step outside to catch him. My eyes track to the back of his dark head, wild curls unfurling from his tall frame. Even taller than mine. He bounds down the street, his long coat billowing in cadence with his gazelle-like stride. A primal wind gnaws at my back. Oddly, as the distance increases, the strength of his pull grows.

(The ongoing serialized version of The Stylist can be found on Kindle Vella.)

A Trip to Key West

Pauline Hayton

I did it on impulse. Two years ago. After I'd caught Bob, partner of three years, in bed with another man. After that I'd returned home from my shift at the hospital to an apartment stripped of all Bob's belongings. Another knife in the gut moment. I needed to do something to cheer myself up after his devastating betrayal. Shocked by the coldness of THE END, I took several deep breaths, lit some incense to cleanse the rooms of any of Bob's remaining energy, and took a Boston lager from the fridge. I sat on my small balcony, brooding. I deserved better. Why waste energy weeping over a broken heart caused by a man who had so quickly taken up with a new lover. Time to move on.

I raised the bottle of beer. "I'll drink to that. Here's to a new life and a trip to Key West."

With suitcase and diving gear in the back of the Highlander, I drove to the Keys to enjoy the festivities of the Key West Gay Pride Parade. I hadn't booked a hotel, but took it as a good omen when, unbelievably, I entered the La Concha Hotel and Spa and discovered that only minutes before a guest had checked out because of a family emergency. I signed in, picked up some brochures of things to do in Key West, then went for a stroll along Duval Street, where the parade would take place in a couple of days.

The hotel receptionist told me the Bourbon Street Pub, also on Duval Street, was a good place for watching the parade. I found it clean and busy. Out back was a pool and large bar where clothing was optional, which I found surprising after living in staid Naples for three and a half years. Boston lager in hand, I found a table and studied the brochures—dolphin encounters, no; kayaking, diving and snorkeling, possibly. I'd brought my diving gear. Maybe I'd rent a boat.

The boisterous antics of swimmers playing water polo and bar patrons cheering them on caused me to look up. A muscular, blond guy caught my eye. He seemed to be the center of attention, seemed to have a lot of friends. He was naked when he emerged from the pool, but had tan lines and lily-white buttocks. I watched him dry himself. He radiated an expansive, confident energy. Not being particularly outgoing myself, I envied the man's hearty bursts of laughter. He looked to be in his mid-forties, older than me. I wished I was in the man's group of friends instead of sitting alone on the sidelines.

A hand touched my shoulder. "Mind if I join you?" The bloated, soft-bellied man sat down, not waiting for an answer. "I've not seen you on the island before and I would have noticed. You're so handsome. You don't live here, do you?"

"No, just visiting."

"From?'

"Naples."

I wanted company but this guy was hitting on me, leering at me, eyeing my muscular thighs.

"You by yourself?"

"Yes—and I'm OK with that."

The man touched my knee. "You sure about that?"

"I'm sure."

The man stood, glared down his nose at me, then with a toss of his head, turned and wandered off, scanning the room for another possible encounter.

My grumbling stomach let me know I needed to eat. I looked at my watch. Breakfast had been seven hours ago. I took one last look at the fun-loving crowd then left to find a cafe.

I spent the following morning wandering around the Street Fair, where I bought several bright, rainbow-colored T-shirts. Next stop was the 7 Artists & Friends art gallery to buy a painting to remind me of my visit to Key West, and also fill one of the empty spaces on the walls left when Bob took his pictures with him. A watercolor of a painted-pink, wooden house caught my eye. It took my breath away with nostalgia for Jamaica. I touched the frame, a caress really. A young woman with frizzy, red hair approached.

"You like this painting?"

"Yes. It reminds me of my Granny's shack in Jamaica, at least, after I found a half-used can of pink paint. I brushed it all over the front of her home as high up as I could reach. The picture even has a cat and a hen sitting near the front door. It brings back happy memories. I'll take it."

"And I'm happy to sell it to you as long as you know my painting is of a house in Key West. It's not in Jamaica."

"You painted this? Well, the important thing is I'll have one painting but two sets of memories — my childhood in Jamaica and my first visit to Key West."

After lunch, I arrived at the Dive Center, where I'd booked an afternoon's diving at the reef, hoping to take photos of tropical fish. That evening, I planned to call in at Bourbon Street Pub for a nightcap, watch the male dancers, listen to the music and maybe see Blond Guy, who had lifted my spirits with his laughter, sparkling eye and vitality. He was a man who seemed to live life to the fullest.

Blond Guy didn't show, but I still enjoyed the lively energy in the bar before walking, a little the worse for wear, back to my hotel.

Sunday, the parade did not start until five. I spent the morning swimming in La Concha's pool and drinking a classic Jamba Juice made with mango, passion fruit, pineapple and non-fat yogurt. After showering, I dressed in one of my new jazzy T-shirts and went looking for a place to eat. I chose Mo's, where a meal of Caribbean creole chicken followed by Key Lime pie satisfied my hunger. I was about to pay and leave when Blond Guy, in a flamboyant, Hawaiian shirt, entered with three friends. Feeling a sudden fluttering in my stomach, I ordered another coffee and hoped the place would not fill up too quickly or I would have felt obliged to drink up and leave — and I didn't want to. There was something about the blond man that attracted me.

The group sat at the next table. Blond Guy was sitting where he could see my face. Every time I took a peek at him, I found him staring at me.

"Enjoying Gay Pride Week?" Blond Guy asked, with a hint of a German accent.

"Yes, first time I've been."

"Didn't I see you the other night in Bourbon Street Pub?"

My eyebrows lifted in surprise. "You looked like you were having too much fun to notice me."

His voice soft and seductive, Blond Guy said, "A handsome man like you stands out in a crowd."

Blond Guy's friends turned to look at me. My face felt hot. Oh God! Was I blushing?

I gulped down my coffee and stood up. "Pleasure meeting you."

"I'm Gunter and you are. . . ?

"Tyrus."

"Where do you live, Tyrus?"

"Naples."

Gunter pulled out a business card and held it out to me. "So do I. My friends and I are in the parade, but maybe I'll see you tonight at Bourbon Street Pub?"

I took the card, my heart beating loudly, and looked at it. "Mixers?"

"It's my gay bar in Naples. If we miss one another tonight, I'd like you to come by sometime."

At five, I was on the balcony at the Bourbon Street Pub. To the beat of tom-tom drums, the parade commenced with a police car leading the way followed by vehicles containing the commissioner, the mayor, and other town officials. People in purple shirts walked alongside throwing handfuls of candy to the crowds. Rainbows decorated most of the other vehicles in the parade. Floats carried dancing men wearing hula skirts. Then I saw Gunter. He was shirtless, wearing hippy necklets and bicycle-style shorts covered in rainbows. He was sitting high up on the back seat of an E-Type convertible that was decorated with rainbow ribbons. As the car passed, Gunter leapt from the vehicle and danced around the vehicle to the 1980s song "We Are Family." It was mesmerizing to watch him tossing his head to the beat, flicking his thick mane, seductively teasing people on the sidewalk who cheered him on during his uninhibited performance. A twinge of light-heartedness lifted my sadness.

I was tempted to spend the evening at the Bourbon Street Pub to see the man I was drawn to, Blond Guy with a personality that seemed bigger than the Empire State Building. But I decided against it. I really wasn't ready for any kind of involvement just yet. Instead, I watched the sunset at Mallory Square.

Next morning, on my way out of town, I visited Papa's Pilar Rum Distillery, departing with three bottles of rum. I was already picturing myself on my small balcony, sipping Papa's Pilar rum, thinking about the wonderful Blond Guy I would soon meet again when I called in at Mixers.

Manhunter

Pauline Hayton

George brought the supper tray to the den where his employer, Mrs. Mitchell, had settled down to watch Downton Abbey.

"Take the night off, George. I won't be needing you anymore today. If you do go out, be sure to set the alarm."

George whistled cheerfully as he hurried to his servant's apartment over the garage and changed into polo shirt and jeans. He was looking forward to a spot of relaxation; it had been a while since he'd had time off. Exiting the exclusive millionaires' subdivision where he lived, it was only a short drive in his Mini Cooper S.

There were about twenty people in Ray's bar and casual dining place when he arrived. Four were sitting at the bar, but they weren't the people he was hoping to see. Louise, the well-tattooed young bartender with short, spiky hair, approached as he took a seat at the bar.

She smiled warmly. "The usual, George?"

"Sure."

She placed a Yuengling and a glass in front of him. "Don't tell me this is the most exciting thing you could be doing on your night off."

"Wouldn't want to miss an opportunity to see your lovely smile and ravishing good looks, Louise."

She laughed and shook her head at their private joke, knowing they both preferred their own sex.

"Hank and the Prof were in three nights ago. I don't know if they'll be in tonight."

She was referring to George's favorite people to have discussions with. Hank was a well-known television personality and the Prof, aka Tony Reiner, a bearded Harvard philosophy professor, who escaped to Naples whenever he could. Both gave George a run for his money when they debated various subjects. George liked that they helped him keep his mind sharp and that he could keep up with them thanks to his eclectic reading habits.

George always enjoyed a visit to Ray's, even on a quiet night. Situated close to the beach, it was a hangout for both the rich and the average Joe who felt at home surrounded by ship's wheels, fishing nets, portholes, and nautical charts. It was a place to relax, be anonymous. Well-known personalities frequently dropped in. Dress was casual. One multi-millionaire, even lowered the standard on what was casual. He smiled at George as he passed by on his way out. George had never seen him in anything but faded T-shirts and frayed shorts. It was Louise who had informed him the man had made millions creating and then selling a popular computer app. George designated himself in the ordinary category of people who hung out at Ray's. Rather than sit in a booth, he preferred sitting at the copper-topped bar where he often ended up discussing world events, history, and news with other patrons.

Whenever someone entered, he looked up, hoping it would be one of his friends, but neither made an appearance. As he waited, George drank a beer and made small-talk with Louise when she wasn't busy serving.

Halfway through his beer, a small, trim blonde in her late fifties came and sat next to him. She struggled to get up on the high bar stool. Taking his arm for leverage, she giggled. "Excuse me. I don't mean to be impertinent."

George helped her up. "No problem."

She finally settled on the stool and hung her purse on the hook under the bar top. "Thank you for being kind. I'm June."

George held out his hand. "George."

She looked around the room and along the bar then smiled at him. He knew this look. Tonight, she was hunting and she had selected him as the prey. "Are you alone? I wouldn't want to intrude."'

He had been through this scenario numerous times. Sometimes it was a female wolfpack on the hunt when he was with friends and sometimes it was a lone wolf as now. Lonely women looking for that special man for them—a man comfortably well off, in good health or so decrepit he would soon kick the bucket. He must have almost no family to fight with over the will when he died. And if they were fortunate, he would be fun and kind and able to perform in bed if they so wished. George knew the drill. Pity she wasn't astute enough to know or even consider that he was unsuitable game for her hunt.

"Yes, I'm alone. My friends aren't here tonight."

The conversation lapsed. She looked at him expectantly.

George smiled to himself. "Can I buy you a drink?"

"Vodka martini, please."

Then she began; he knew how it would go.

"Do you live around here?"

"Yes, in Bay Colony."

"Bay Colony? It's so nice in there." Delighted, she snuggled up to his arm.

Oh-oh, she's liquored-up. Probably been to several bars already to try her luck.

She patted her cemented-in-place hair. "My condo's in Park Shore. Are you married? Divorced?"

"Single right now."

She laughed coyly and gave a gentle push to his arm. "But you're so good-looking. I'm sure you must be very popular with women. I bet you have a girlfriend."

"No girlfriend."

"So, you're all alone. It's sad to be alone. At least, that's what I've found."

"Divorced?"

"No, widowed. My husband was killed in a car crash two years ago."

"I'm sorry to hear that. I guess it takes a while to adjust to being alone when you've been part of a couple for some years."

She smiled at him, fluttering her eyelashes. "You're so understanding."

George was almost ready to call it a day, but he wanted to see if June's finale would be any different from other female hunters. He pointed to her glass. "Would you like another?"

"Yes, please."

George caught Louise's eye and pointed to their empty glasses. She refilled their drinks, raised her eyebrows and looked askance at George as if to say, "What are you doing?" George raised his eyebrows in return and gave a small shrug.

June took a sip of her drink. "Are you retired?"

"No, I still work for a living."

"Let me guess. You're a lawyer."

George shook his head.

"You run your own business."

Again, George shook his head.

June playfully shoved his arm. "Okay, I give in. What do you do?"

"I'm a butler."

George had to give June her due. She managed not to recoil. She continued smiling, made small talk as she drank her vodka martini as fast as she could without appearing unlady-like. Then, having remembered she had to see a friend, bade him goodnight and thanks for a pleasant evening.

He watched her totter carefully toward the door, then he turned back to the bar and pulled out his wallet. Louise brought over his bar tab.

"Didn't take you long to drive her away."

His voice dripping with sarcasm, George said, "Well, that went splendidly."

Louise put her hands on her hips and smiled brightly. "If you say so."

He snickered. Bum, bum, bum, his hand tapped the beat on the bar as he hummed a Freddie Mercury song: "Another one Bites the Dust."

Louise chuckled. "Sarcasm becomes you."

Grinning, George paid his bill, saluted Louise, and left.

Hey Doc!
[A true story.]

Jennie Weckelman

The wrinkle-faced little fellow held out both hands, palms up. "Hey, Doc, you got...," he mumbled in a patois. I couldn't quite make it out, and hesitated in mid-stride, looking down into the dark, impish face. Later I discovered he was near to forty, but his size and demeanor were very child-like. His gap-toothed smile was so sunny it made me smile. His vocation was panhandling, and he was a really likeable beggar with dark leathery skin and even darker brown eyes.

Disliking public scenes, my husband kept walking. "He just wants a handout," Mike said over his shoulder, obviously displeased and embarrassed. I didn't have the heart to compound Mike's awkwardness by disagreeing, so did not place anything in the little outstretched hand. Turning away to follow Mike, I caught a glimpse of brief disappointment on the small man's face before he instantly recovered and flashed that smile again. "Another time would be better," I said to myself, "when Mike isn't around." Maybe I could get to know this intriguing person by returning. Afterall, this was only our first day on the island of Montserrat, set in jewel-like seas, so close to the equator that days were evenly distributed between darkness and light. Intuitively, I knew I would find Heydoc, as everyone called him, on the waterfront most days.

The odd little man was there nearly every day, always in the same general location, smiling that huge, too-big-for-his-face grin, and asking for a handout in his abbreviated English. He never seemed to mind when people turned him down. "Aw-wight, Doc," was all he would say with a downward glance and shy smile.

The little man's physical being was inconsistent. The thick wrinkles on his face folded in upon themselves when he smiled, like a human Shar Pei. They made him look older than his estimated forty years. His body, on the other hand, reminded me of a toddler. It was out of proportion to his head, smaller, and he would seesaw from foot to foot when he walked, his too-short arms swaying, his too-short legs part of his overall height, somewhere under five-foot.

We were to live on the thirty-nine-square-mile Caribbean Island for eighteen months, two teenage sons in tow, their education through the mail, while my husband frustrated himself adding another doctorate to his credentials at this carefully selected Caribbean medical college. First pharmacy, then veterinary and now human medicine. And then there would be three more years of clerk and internships, we knew not where, yet. We hoped for the States, but Ireland and England became the only options in the end.

Television was a luxury on the island, and none for us; personal computers were not yet truly portable nor even prevalent; there was limited phone service, puny stores, and only two or three restaurants. Mail from the States was slow and we had only one car, rented for the duration. Weather-beaten two-room shacks predominated, scattered over the hillsides or clustered in tiny villages with quaint names. The capital and main port, Plymouth, had concrete and block structures with only a few of those being two-storied. The volcano loomed, steam shrouded, smelling of sulphur, most days. The whole island reminded me of the deep south of the U.S. in the 1950's, run-down and unambitious.

The other students were younger, or from a different culture, some with younger families, ours were nearly grown. There was really little time for socializing anyway because of a tight budget, lack of transportation, my husband's wariness of the natives, and the widely scattered housing. The students, including my husband, were up to their ears with study and financial worries; their spouses were busy balancing the budget, caring and schooling their young children or scouting for food. This was a medical school of warp speed, study, study, study! I was at loose ends and could not fill my time with planning for the next major move because we did not know where we would go yet or how long it might take.

Obtaining food in a quantity sufficient for a husband and two teenagers meant a treasure hunt on Montserrat every week and cooking from scratch every day. No McDonalds here! No wide-aisled, shelf-laden grocery stores either. No sir! Just a few shelves in a shack, sparsely stocked with canned goods, one freezer in the back with Grade C frozen chickens (if the boat came in) and an open-air market. That market swarmed with flies on the hanging meat and a small selection of seasonal fruits and vegetables, some of which I had never seen before and had no idea how to handle. If you needed eggs, good luck. It took time and friends to know where to find them.

Although a sovereign nation, Montserrat is part of the United Kingdom. A complicated political form with a U.K. appointed Governor and compensatory payments for each Montserratian, referred to as "the dole". Perhaps as many as 3,000 citizens lived on the island permanently at that time, many "on the dole" or at least eligible for it. Another 2,000 or so lived in the U.S. and three times that many in England. Every year, in season, home-comers and vacationers swelled the population to 10,000 or more and Carnival filled the streets every night in December for a week of jumping and gyrating humans parading behind flat-bed trucks upon which a band played.

The island, devoid long ago of the Arawak and Carib populations, was subsequently settled by a few outcast or impoverished Irish who worked alongside the enslaved Africans brought to work on the sugar, and later, pineapple plantations. These latter-day, predominantly black natives, spoke a good English, sprinkled with the occasional tribal African word, and delivered with a slight Irish brogue. A few came from nearby islands where French was spoken with a rhythm and words of their own.

I tried to find out more about Heydoc, beyond the fact that all the medical students and their spouses called him that due to his own oft-repeated words, but no one knew more. Here was a man who lived in the moment. He seemed to have no past, and he showed no outward sign of wanting to leave a mark on the world for the future. He always approached respectfully, if a bit persistently, head down, then tilted upwards at a sly angle revealing that happy grin. "Hey Doc, you got something for me?" I finally deciphered.

He appeared to be a dwarf and I would like to have known his story. Even though I inquired to many, most knew nothing of him and seemed uninterested. Natives seemed reluctant to speak about him, whether from lack of knowledge or adverse to gossiping about their neighbor to a stranger. I never knew. Even my housekeeper, Agnes, who's twice a week labors came with the rented house, would not, or could not, enlighten me. She had grown up in the same village and she supposed they were about the same age, but with a shrug, she never said more. She did not even know his real name.

Most days Heydoc took a forty-five-minute ride on the bus from his native village of St. Johns, at the northern tip of the island, to Plymouth, at the southern tip. Heydoc spent the daylight hours pacing the waterfront or roaming the cool shadows of the loggia that fronted the post office, with graceful arches and outer wall open to the elements. At lunch he managed to gnaw nourishment from a loaf of French bread with only a few teeth.

The most remarkable thing about him, though, was his great big smile, which appeared to be born of contentment; and although his occupation was looked down upon by many, his work seemed essential somehow and he obviously enjoyed it. Putting a few coins into that leathery little hand made me feel useful, as I thought it must have made others feel. He smiled expansively when a coin was put into his hand, we all smiled back, big, every time.

It was strange to me that he could live in this very small country for forty years without having made a stir or story. His cheerful acceptance of a simple lifestyle was a glaring contrast to my boredom with living in that same place.

The weather, though seemingly perfect at first, became boring. In fact, it was relentlessly perfect ten months of the year. Each day brought sunshine but buckets of rain filled every night. The strong trade winds were constant, unnerving, and annoying. A nearly empty black-sand beach, towering volcano and the sapphire-blue ocean surrounding it all was breathtaking, though. It should have been the proverbial paradise, but there was not much to engage one's mind. Thank goodness for the library! Endless books, countless games of scrabble and swimming in the pool or ocean went on day after day while my husband's attentions were concentrated on study every waking hour.

Accustomed to striving for something every day and setting goals for tomorrow back in the States, I felt adrift, suspended in time between the past and the future. It is not as easy as it looks to live in the present, even in paradise. I tried. After a while I imagined the little man's smile to be scolding me and hiding a secret I could not grasp. Pondering then and continually since, I find there to be not one, but many possible answers to that enigma. All of them highly individualized. Most of all I wondered if there was something wrong with my culture --the one I had known all my life. The one ripe with avarice, gluttony and rushing here and there. Had we all missed something?

Two years after we left the island, enroute first to England, later to home in Missouri, Hurricane Hugo roared over the island and a couple years after that, the volcano erupted viciously and ninety percent of what we had known was destroyed, several people dying. Heydoc was one of them. He smiles only in memory now. Besides the haunting whispers to enjoy life each day, he left another mark on me. That smile!

photo provided by Janice Teakell,
photo editing by Joanne Simon Tailele

Snow Angel

Joanne Simon Tailele

Tara Simon did not believe in miracles, but she did believe in a good story. If she could land one exceptional article, the Chicago Tribune senior editor would have no choice but to grant her request for a weekly column of her own. She'd paid her dues, bid her time, started at the very bottom of the journalism pool. This was her chance. It had to work.

The snow had picked up from a white dusting to heavy, thick flakes that clumped together as they fell, creating a feeling of walking through a snowball fight. Visibility was poor at best as Tara made her way into the Children's Cancer Center of Chicago. She stomped her feet to dislodge the two-inch coating of white stuck to her brown knee-high boots. The warmth of the reception area quickly melted the crystals affixed to her long red hair and her thick eyelashes.

"I'm here to see Meredith Carter." Tara flashed her journalism badge and a toothy smile. "Her mother agreed to the interview."

A nurse in Scooby-Doo scrubs eyed her identification. She did not return the smile. "Meredith is still recovering. She needs her rest."

"Of course," said Tara. "I promise to only stay a few minutes. She is a very lucky girl, isn't she?"

"Luck had nothing to do with it," said Nurse Scooby-Doo. "It's nothing short of a miracle. Five minutes." She spread her fingers before tapping on the utilitarian watch on her wrist. "Room 1403."

Tara nodded her thanks and hurried down the sterile green hallway with colorful Disney posters adorning the walls. She found room 1403 following the white-gloved Mickey Mouse hand directions at each hall crossing. She tapped lightly on the partially opened door.

A woman, appearing not much older than Tara, blond hair pulled back in a ponytail, sat on the edge of the high hospital bed holding a child's small hand. She looked up at Tara and smiled.

"Hello, Mrs. Carter? I'm Tara Simon, from the Tribune. Is this a good time?" Tara took in the child in the bed. Dwarfed by the size of the hospital bed, she looked tinier than the eight-years-old in her preliminary report. Only her wide, round eyes, a startling blue, contrasted the white sheets, the pale skin, the shiny bald head.

"Yes, please come in," Angela Carter said. She smiled back at her daughter. "Meredith, this is the lady I told you about who wants to tell your story. Is that okay with you?"

The blue eyes lit up the room, sparkling from the overhead florescent lighting. "Sure Mommy. I want to tell my story."

Tara pulled up a chair on the other side of the bed from Mrs. Carter. "Thank you, Meredith. I am sure lots of people would like to hear it. Can you tell me what happened?"

"The Snow Angel came and made me all better," she said, beaming at her mother.

"The Snow Angel I don't understand. Did she come into your room?"

"No, silly. She came to the window. When it was snowing, just like today."

Tara looked toward the window. Beyond the thick blanket of snow on the window ledge, she could see nothing but the tops of the trees, now heavy laden in clear crystals of ice. "How is that possible? You are on the 6th floor of this building?"

Meredith shrugged. She pointed to the window. "She was right there."

Tara looked up at Mrs. Carter. Tears were streaming down

her cheeks but a smile reached from ear to ear.

"They said it was only a matter of days we had left with her. The cancer, it had metastasized to her blood stream. There was nothing else they could do. I hadn't left her bedside in days. But I fell asleep. I awoke with Meredith calling my name. She hadn't spoken in weeks. Now look at her."

Other than being extremely pale and the lack of hair, Mrs. Carter was right. Meredith looked the picture of health. "I don't understand," said Tara.

"Nobody does. Meredith says the Snow Angel woke her up, calling to her from the window and told her she would be okay now. . . and she is. It's a miracle."

The child was clearly having a hallucination. This had to be one of those rare, unexplained medical phenomena. "Can you tell me what the Snow Angel looked like?" Tara asked.

"Oh yes. She had long blond hair that curled around her face and poked out from a white furry hood on her head. She was very pretty with sparkly green eyes. She told me not to be afraid anymore and to wake up Mommy and tell her I was all better."

"Aren't you a lucky little girl," Tara said. She wanted to believe, but her brain couldn't wrap around it.

"I'm sure you don't want to believe it," said Mrs. Carter. "But the doctors can't explain it either. The cancer is all gone . . . all of it." She squeezed the child's hand.

Nurse Scooby-Doo stuck her head in the door. "Time's up. You'll have to leave now."

"Of course." Tara turned to Meredith and her mother. "Thank you for telling me your story." She took the elevator to the front entrance and looked up at the 6th floor. She spotted the one next to the big oak tree. Meredith must have seen a shadow from the trees and her mind played a trick on her. She hurried to her car, anxious to get back to her laptop to write up the story. One little girl's imagination and an unexplained recovery was probably not enough to win that coveted spot on the paper. But it was heartwarming and not the end of the story.

The next day, Tara boarded a plane to Detroit Medical Center to interview six-year-old Darian Montgomery. He'd been in a terrible car accident and had been declared brain dead. Until the night of a huge snowstorm when he woke up and claimed a Snow Angel had visited him at his window and told him to tell his father he was going to be okay.

And three days after Darian, eleven-year-old Amanda Fisher woke up from the Cleveland Clinic's medically induced coma after she had been burned over fifty percent of her body. She told her grandmother the Snow Angel had come and said her skin would grow back. The doctors watched it heal right before their eyes. Within three weeks, she had new skin and not a single scar to show from the fire.

Tara followed each lead. She looked for ways the families could have schemed this for publicity. No connections. The children and families did not know each other. They lived in different towns, had different injuries and illnesses. Different ethnic and economic backgrounds. But the one thing in common was the snow, and the little girl with the blond curls and fur hood who appeared at their windows. Tara asked a sketch artist to draw what each child saw from their descriptions. Each picture was identical.

Tara landed the promotion she'd coveted and the weekly column. But her focus had changed since the Snow Angel. Instead of chasing the prestige and almighty dollar, her column consisted of one subject. The Possibility of Miracles.

The Cat Murderer

Joanne Simon Tailele

Gertrude had one love over the past ten years since she'd become a widow. Sebastian, her white Persian. The idea of leaving him at home to visit her terminally ill sister, Josephine, was almost more than she could bear. But Josephine was highly allergic to cats and this was most likely the last time Gertrude would see sister Jo in this life.

"I'll watch him," said Annabelle, Gertrude's next-door neighbor. Annabelle and Gertrude had lived next door to each other for thirty years, had seen each other through child-raising, college days, children's weddings, and widowhood. If anyone understood Sebastian's idiosyncrasies, it was Annabelle. She was one of the few people that could visit without Sebastian diving under the bed.

Gertrude stroked Sebastian's long fur as he lay on her lap, purring with a perpetual frown on his flat little face. "What do you think, baby boy? Should we let Auntie Annie take care of you for a few days?"

Annabelle tsked at her and reached over to pat the top of his head. Sebastian hissed, spring from Gertrude's lap and darted into the bedroom and under the bed.

Gertrude frowned. "He probably won't let you pet him."

"Maybe not, but he'll like me better once he realizes I'm feeding him and changing his box. You go, visit Josephine, we will get along fine."

Two days later, Gertrude reluctantly boarded a plane and took off for Minnesota. She filled her handbag with pictures of her "baby boy" and said a silent prayer he wouldn't hate her too much for deserting him. Cats could be so peculiar.

Once at the hospital, Gertrude could clearly see that Josephine was in decline and had little interest in Sebastian's pictures. They had little to talk about. The long-term distance in their relationship was not getting better. All Gertrude's thoughts were about Sebastian and the cat's antics were of no interest to Josephine. Gertrude checked in on Annabelle and Sebastian every day and was more than ready to go home at the end of the week.

The second she stepped into the house, Gertrude squealed with delight and scooped up Sebastian. He didn't snuggle against her neck when she picked him up as usual and quickly squirmed away. Gertrude felt her heart drop. "Are you mad at me for leaving you alone?"

She turned and noticed a beautiful blue ceramic vase containing gorgeous butter-yellow lilies on the table. Oh, how lovely. That wasn't necessary. She should be the one bringing gifts to Annabelle for taking care of Sebastian, not the other way around.

She called Annabelle and invited her over for tea and to thank her for the flowers. "Was Sebastian acting strange to you? He hasn't come out from under the bed since I got home. It was so unlike him. "

"He'll come around. You know how finicky cats can be. He's been listless since yesterday. I figured he was missing you." said Annabelle.

They finished their tea while Annabelle caught Gertrude up on the latest neighborhood gossip. Gertrude didn't want to hear gossip. Her thoughts were on Sebastian.

Annabelle headed out the door to her own home. Gertrude leaned over and inhaled the sweet scent of the lily. Sometimes she am too quick to judge people. I truly am blessed to have such a good neighbor. She went on a hunt for Sebastian. He was cowed under the bed between the crates of Christmas decorations. A sour smell caused Gertrude to wrinkle her nose. Then she saw it. Two welcome home presents for her: a pile of runny feces and another glob of cat vomit. "Oh baby-boy, are you sick? Come out here and let me take care of you." Sebastian moved farther back out of her reach.

Gertrude got the cleaner and crawled clumsily under the bed to clean up the messes. Then she unpacked, put some fresh cat food out for Sebastian and made herself a sandwich. Typically, he would come running at the sound of the can opening. Not this time. Two hours later, he had still not come out to eat.

She crawled back under the bed and moved away the crates so she could reach Sebastian. She pulled him from under the bed, and sitting on the floor, laid him across her lap. His head flopped to the side and lay limp in her arms. Alarm triggered a pounding heart in her chest. "Baby-boy, what's wrong?" She stroked his fur, but he did not purr.

Something was definitely wrong. Gertrude couldn't wait and worry any longer. She called the vet. He told her to bring him in right away. It didn't take any effort to get Sebastian in the carrier, which was a sure sign that things were not normal.

Dr. Thompson examined Sebastian. "He is really dehydrated. I'd like to keep him overnight, put him on an intravenous fluid drip, take a blood sample, and give him some sucralfate."

Gertrude's hand clutched her throat. "Why? What is wrong with him?"

"I can't be 100% sure. He may have eaten something he shouldn't. Maybe a bad can of cat food. The blood test will tell us more. We'll know more by tomorrow."

"I don't understand."

"What have you fed him lately?" the veterinarian asked.

"I . . . I've been away. But I gave my neighbor his food – the same cat food he's eaten for years."

"Well, ask your neighbor again if she fed him anything new."

Gertrude pulled into the garage, suspicion of Annabelle building every second. Had she made a mistake trusting Annabelle with Sebastian? Hesitating, she debated going next door and confronting her. With a nod, she walked across the grass. She knocked on the door. No answer. She peaked through the side light. No lights, no motion. She must have gone out.

Gertrude trudged back across the lawn and into her too quiet house. No Sebastian greeting her with his loud meow. No clang of his bell from his collar dinging against his water bowl. She undressed and climbed into bed. Sleep was impossible.

Gertrude closed her eyes and could swear she felt Sebastian's footsteps across the blanket. But of course, he wasn't there. What if he died? She couldn't deal with losing another loved one so soon after her husband's passing. And what about Annabelle? If she really did this, how could she ever forgive her? Could she live next door to a cat murderer?

Dr. Thompson called about nine a.m. the next morning. Sebastian was doing better. The fluids and meds had helped. Gertrude could take him home. Gertrude hung up the phone and collapsed in tears, burying her face in her hands.

At the vet's office, Sebastian loudly greeted her, pawing at the cage to get out. She released him and cuddled him in her arms. He purred loudly in her ear. "So, doc, what happened to him?"

Dr. Thompson looked at her sheepishly. "Well, the blood work indicates that Sebastian was poisoned — "

"POISONED," she shouted. "Annabelle . . . I knew it." She pulled Sebastian closer to her.

Dr. Thompson's cell phone rang. He glanced at it and raised a finger. "One minute. I have to take this call, Gertrude."

She slipped Sebastian back into his carrier and left, not waiting for his call to complete. A sick feeling settled in the pit of her stomach. On the way home, she thought about the relationship between Annabelle and Sebastian. She wouldn't have really done anything on purpose to harm him, would she? Her mind wandered back to past episodes. Sebastian had torn up Gertrude's vegetable garden last summer. Annabelle was not at all happy about that. And he did have a habit of presenting his prizes of dead field mice and baby birds on her front doorstep.

The car was barely in park when Gertrude flew out the door and stomped across the lawn to Annabelle's. She banged on the door with her fist. Annabelle appeared, wiping her hand on a dish towel and smiling until she saw Gertrude's scowl.

"What's wrong?" She held the door for Gertrude to enter the foyer.

"You poisoned Sebastian!" Gertrude crossed her arms across her chest. "Dr. Thompson says he was p-o-i-s-e-n-e-d." She stretched out the word. "You were the only one with him. You never did like him, did you? You hate the presents he leaves you. But this Annabelle . . . I can't believe you would do this. I thought we were friends." Gertrude swung the front door open hard, letting it bang against the foyer wall. "If he dies, Annabelle, I swear . . ." She did not finish the sentence but stomped across the lawn.

Annabelle called after her. "No, no, no. I swear. I only fed him the cat food you gave me."

The phone was ringing when she stepped into her house. The caller ID said it was Dr. Thompson. She grabbed the receiver. "Doc? What is it? More bad news?"

"No," he said. "Sorry for the interruption with the phone call. You left without letting me finish. Yes, Sebastian was poisoned, but I believe it was an accident. I found lily leaves in his stool. It appears he was eating the leaves from the plant. Most people don't know that cats are allergic to a lot of different house plants."

Gertrude's head swung to look at the plant on the table. "The lily? Annabelle did leave me a present of a lily plant. But you don't think it was on purpose?"

"I highly doubt it. Especially if she is not a cat owner. Did you know lilies were poisonous to Sebastian?"

"Well, no. I thought it was a lovely gift. It's right here on my dining room table. Oh my. Thank you for explaining Dr. Thompson."

She hung up and looked out the window. Annabelle was standing in her front yard, looking as though she'd lost her best friend. Of course, she almost had.

Gertrude laid Sebastian in his bed and headed outside, carrying the lily plant. She walked over and handed it to Annabelle.

"Keep it," said Annabelle. "I swear I would never hurt Sebastian. Is he okay?"

A small struggle ensued as the two women tried to force the plant back into the other's hands.

"Stop," said Gertrude, shoving the plant once more and letting go so Annabelle had no choice but to accept the plant. "I am so sorry. I owe you a huge apology. I know you didn't poison Sebastian. But he liked your gift a little too much. He ate some of the leaves, and they can be lethal to cats."

Annabelle stepped back, dropping the plant so the ceramic pot shattered on the ground. "Oh no. I didn't know. I never would have given it to you."

Gertrude put her arms out and accepted Annabelle

into a hug. "I know, dear friend. I never should have doubted you. I'm so sorry."

The two women went arm-in-arm back into Gertrude's house. She put on the tea kettle and they sat at the small round table. Sebastian stealthily crept across the floor and jumped into Annabelle's lap.

"Oh, hello there. Are we friends now?" She laughed and stroked his soft fur. "and no more plants for you, young man."

It's Not Your Time

Jean Duling

Whoa, I am coming back to consciousness. Hospital sounds buzz and beep. Nurses rush to the patient in the bed next to me. From the station outside the door there is soft chatter. The loudspeaker calls Dr. Golding to room 301.

Okay now, what is this? What about that great meeting with my peacemaker? God talking to me. Why did he say? "It is not your time, Jean." He has to know the pain of the past week. This loss of some of my eyesight, the difficulty in walking and admission to the hospital?

I opened my eyes to see Dr. Golding, the neurologist. He asked, "Well, how are you feeling?"

I never liked to answer how I am feeling. I didn't seem to know. When I was in a serious automobile accident in college and my father visited me in the hospital every day and asked how I was. I said "K" even though I certainly was not all right.

"I'm okay." I hesitated to tell him of my meeting with the great beyond. Would he even believe me?

After examining me he said, "The steroids do strange things to some people. The heart doctor will be in to check your heart again. Now you just rest."

"What does he think I am going to do, run a marathon around the hospital?" It was just fine to close my eyes and reflect on what had happened. *Somehow Daddy had been there.* "I miss you Daddy," I whimpered. *You have been gone only a few months. I was going to heaven to be with you. Why are you gone? Will I ever stop grieving? Why did God say "It's not your time Jean, you have more to do?"*

Whatever do I need to get done? Teaching days are gone. Working in the card shop is fine, yet what does anyone need me for? There are always other people to work – People much more apt to sell lots of merchandise. Will I ever be strong enough to walk? To work? Even to think again?

This Multiple Sclerosis thing has knocked me for a loop.

A Nurse took my blood pressure. I asked, "What is this thing?"

The nurse fired back, "You are on a heart monitor!"

Why don't I just shut up and sleep? Because this is not me. I am full of questions. Of course, I have no idea what they are talking about. Yet I ask. They respond. I forget. One thing is for sure, my brain seems really diminished since this onset of what they say is Multiple Sclerosis. Who knows how long this has been going on, too? This spell seems like an eternity already. Yet surely this isn't the first episode. They just never identified it.

In came Dr. Carlson, the heart doctor. "Wow, good to see you sitting up now and wide awake. How are you feeling?"

Looking over at the calendar on the wall, I realized it was Valentine's Day and I was in the cardiac wing. I joked, "This is an appropriate place for a hopeless romantic on Valentine's Day." After Dr. Carlson left, the phone rang. It was my osteopath, Dr, King, from up north. What a welcome surprise! My daughter must have called him.

"Jean, tell me how you are doing."

I rattled away about all the things that had gone on for the last few days. I exclaimed, "I'm losing what is left of my brain! I cannot remember diddly-squat. It is lucky I remember I am Jean."

Dr. King soothed me in his usual calm reassuring voice. "Jean, you are not going to hell in a handbasket. You have just accounted for the last four days. You have given me the sequence of events in perfect detail. You are in good hands there."

Dr. King talked the way he always did to help me make sense of my mixed-up life. He is such a great osteopath. He is the only one who understands me. He apologized for the State Retirement System when they would offer no help for me. Other doctors needed to say I was unable to work. Neurologists thought I had a simple concussion, from a fall. I had been forced to leave teaching. Teaching had been my whole life. I finally had the most beautiful classroom. The architect designs for the new addition were perfect for a creative classroom, a delight to this teacher.

Dr. King helped me so much. When the neurologists said they could find nothing, he gave me relief, doing cranial manipulation. Osteopathic medicine became the new topic of study for this patient. His office music relaxed me into an amazing peace. It took time yet within time the vertigo subsided a good deal.

A year after leaving teaching in Maine, Wes and I went to Florida. We had vacationed in Florida for twenty years. Mom and Dad left us a nice condo. How lucky we were! I found work and felt like a reborn person. I was worth something, Yet, what was going to happen now? I had Multiple Sclerosis. No one in the world could understand how I felt!

Wes arrived at the bedside. "Sit down," I commanded. Wes set the rose in the white bud vase on the bed table. He gingerly sat in a chair by my bed and made himself as comfortable as he ever could be in a hospital.

I started to tell my story. "Well, I am here. I wondered what was happening last night and three times I felt I was leaving. It was very peaceful. Lovely "

Nurses' aides and attendants struggled to move the lady next to me. The poor woman groaned. They wheeled her out on a moving bed somewhere. The background people rushed by the door. The loudspeaker quaked again, "Dr. Golding, stat." Everything here made me appreciate the peace of leaving I had experienced all the more.

"Wes, it was wonderful. I met God. *I knew Wes would understand – Wes was a believer, yet would he believe this story?*

"I was looking forward to going with God. Daddy was there." God's voice said, "It is not your time."

"What could I have to do, hon?"

"Be my wife," Wes said so tenderly. How touching! A week before we were considering separating. He was always matter of fact. He showed no emotion. That was Wes. I used to think I was his barometer. When I was depressed, he was, when I was happy, he was. *Did he even believe me, that I met with my peacemaker? Did it really matter? I knew I had met God and I felt happy to return and think about the future. What future? Was I going to be able to walk? Well, if not, could I write and read still?*

I was too tired to do anything now. How could I feel so awful? The library poetry speech "Perseverance Vs Procrastination" was to be Monday night. I certainly felt unable to give a speech in this condition. I was already to give it – so well prepared. The library was going to be the perfect place for it. The other speakers were wonderful. They motivated me. I knew it was going to be good, and all the books of poetry I might have been able to sell. Lying in the carton, in the condo.

Oh, well, does it matter that I could not give the speech? So what if the people aren't going to hear me? I am prepared. I am happy with myself, with my preparation. Maybe I would have fluffed anyway. What if I had made a horrendous mistake? Forgot the prop to show and tell. Oh well.

"What is happening at home? Tell me. Give me a kiss," I commanded.

Wes leaned over and gave me a peck. "The kids called from Maine; Mom (his) called. She is driving south with my sister, Paula. They should be here in a couple of days. We'll get you home and be able to enjoy seeing them. Maybe I'll take some time off from work."

Wes worked for a floor covering place. He and the owner laid tile. Others did carpet work. This was his second year with the company.

"No, Hon, you better keep working Someone has to make money. I am going to be laid up for a while." *Who knows how long? What if I never could go back to work?"*

Suddenly everything started crashing in on me. I thought of the anguishing time when I was in the transition from teaching, wondering if I could return. No one knew how I felt. No one cared. No one was there. I started to cry. "What can I do? I can't do anything."

"Yes, you can, hon. You love to make your cards; you like to write. You can stay home, and I can take care of you."

"I don't want anyone to take care of me. You put me in a nursing home. You are going to have a life!" I retaliated.

"You won't need a nursing home. You have too much drive. You'll be up and walking right away. Now try to get some rest, I've gotta go."

"Oh, you just got here, you are not a visitor. *He hates hospitals. His late father was a Lutheran minister. He visited everyone in the hospitals. Wes insisted that is how his father died – that he picked up some rare disease. Maybe he is right. Maybe his father hadn't died of pneumonia like they said. I should be grateful Wes came. It was Saturday. He should have fun.*

"Thanks for the valentine hon. Go to the bureau in the back bedroom and in the second drawer is your gift."

I bought him a corvette mug from the store some time ago. It was all wrapped. The card I hadn't signed, so I didn't mention that. That was in a separate bag. He could care less about cards anyway.

"Thanks for coming. I love you."

"Ya, bye now."

Oh, how I wish he was coming back tonight. Well, think I will get a little shut eye.

Things whirled for a while until I slept. It was not the end of my life. I have more to do. There is much more to do. I recovered well from this event and at a later date went back to work. It wasn't the end of the world; it was the opening of a new world. Having MS taught me to enjoy life, examine priorities and not worry about the small things. I was becoming more self-educated. I will ever be grateful for this great awakening and this drifting, drifting time and "more to do."

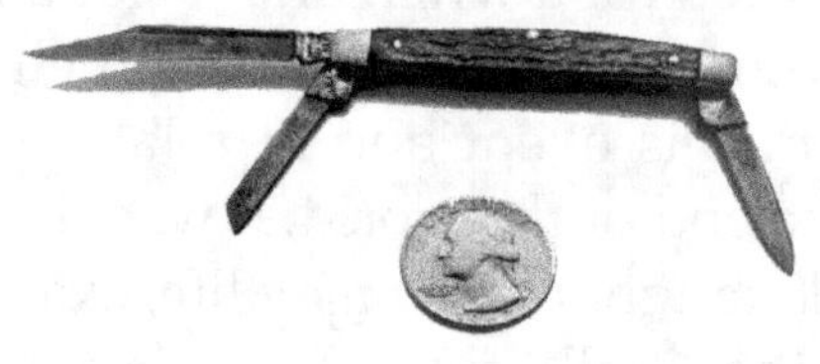

Memento Mori

James Masciarelli

A vintage knife loose in a box of old photographs. Not just any pocketknife, this whittler defies time to a California dreaming summer of love and adventure. A memento of my youth, vivacity and naivete. But the three bladed, old-timer had another purpose. Crime.

We are time travelers that learn, forget, repress, and awaken. A memento reinstates us to time and place with emotion, sensation, choices made. To reminisce over a mere souvenir can trivialize experience. There are usually deeper truths. A grand memento may force us to confront and embrace hard lessons learned. Why else keep it? Why do I keep it?

After surrendering and downsizing from all manner of attachments, why do we still hold mementos? Or fail to remember that some are stuffed away? Perhaps certain items have power for us or against our better selves. We are not discussing hoarding here. That is borderline.

Growing up in a small New England farm town, I was fortunate to develop skills from good jobs, save for college, especially at the local hardware store for contractors and residents long before bubble packs, when customers got exactly the parts and personal services needed—cutting keys, pipes to length, machine threaded, screen doors repaired and windows glazed. Then a summer job in 1967 running heavy equipment to clear and groom a new golf course. I could only imagine being in California, with songs about San Francisco and living for today. My wanderlust would have to wait.

My adventurous elder brother, Gene, surprised me with an invite to summer in San Diego with his family in 1968. My first flight on a jet airliner. I found temporary work through Manpower as a lumper. You show up at a designated corner at 6:30 AM and climb into a stake bed truck with a rough, motley bunch. One fella tosses an empty pint off the truck. We arrive at a white stucco building with a modest sign over the entrance - Italian Spaghetti Company.

A brutal job to unload and lug sacks of flour in the building and up three flights of cement stairs. Smiling Latinas sit at long tables rolling dough, cutting pasta to hang on wood drying racks. Two Mexican bosses ran the place. I became entertainment for the ladies with my heroic pace. Initially. One of them giggled and glanced at me through her long fingers. They had seen this movie before. Two of the guys lasted only 4 hours.

By law, forty-nine-pound floppy flour sacks were deemed a true quarter barrel of 196 pounds. So, one sack per shoulder for a nine-hour shift. No handles. My steps slower, legs burning, body sopping with sweat to make the third floor. No air conditioning, but mercifully some open windows with a light breeze. I lose my grip and a sack slips off my shoulder. Then another. . . and another. They want their money's worth and two sacks at a time is the expectation. By 2 p.m., I switch it up, lug sacks to the second-floor landing, and backtrack one at a time to the third floor. Quitting time finally came and I thought I was done. Last man standing, but they insisted I straighten and restack the whole load on the third floor to save space. My commitment to higher education renewed, but my back has not forgiven me since.

Gene was kind to loan me his Yamaha twin-jet 100cc motorcycle to get around. It was a fun bike but light for speedy drives on four lane highways. I needed wheels and bought a green flathead six, 1948 Plymouth coupe for a hundred bucks. With truck tires and serious mileage. My first modification was to rip out the back seat, put in a plywood platform with a mattress. Then I painted the side rear windows yellow, for privacy and style. Lame, but I'm eighteen. Not a car you would miss. The wild scene at Balboa Park on weekends was said to rival the '67 summer in San Francisco. It was.

I got a lead for a permanent job at the lumber company adjacent to the new San Diego Marine Port terminal, which received heavy timber and finished lumber from Canada. They looked me and the application over, did not ask many questions and offered a great paying union job. I am sun darkened, with a full beard, head bandana, denim shirt and jeans, and size 14 work boots. They did not figure me for a college kid just there for the summer. After a few days of inventory work and moving lumber with a propane forklift, they promoted me to supervisor of the stud loading department. Yup, a real title and step up to drive a three-story high diesel forklift to move massive loads. Climbing up that cage for the first time, I took in the panorama of San Diego Bay, the waterfront, and my adult crew below.

One of the men was about thirty, trim, clean cut, ex-military. Frank? Yes, Frank. I liked his work ethic. I pegged him as a team player with a positive attitude.

After my first week on the job, Frank invited me to go surfing at Imperial Beach near the pier in Oceanside, known for some serious waves and action. Frank was a magnet for women. I was living the dream. Frank taught me how to tackle rollers. Fully spent, with bleeding knees, scrapes, phone numbers and a big smile, we called it a day.

The following week, Frank said his car was in the shop and he needed a ride home Friday after work, we could have a drink on the way. I accepted.

We hit a pool hall that Friday night. We played. I lost. He hustled other players, made a stake, lost it and moved on to another place, rinse and repeat. Frank's eyes were on fire. My gut tightened as I watched the tables and the action. Frank got on a winning streak, paid for my drinks, and kept them coming. No Mas! I struggled to stay awake. Another drink came with his big grin. Now he owed money but doubled down. I was groggy, staggered outside, and passed out in my car.

Saturday morning. I awake when we lurch to a stop in a driveway. I am sprawled in the back of my Plymouth surrounded by bags of cash, coins, tools, and groceries.

"What the...?"

"This is for you." Frank hands me a small pocketknife with a dark bone handle. "Great for jimmying locks, latches, and vending machines. Let's go in, get some coffee."

This cannot be happening. "I am not touching that stuff, Frank."

Frank grabs two of the bags of money, a fresh carton of Marlboros, and snack food. Probably from mom-and-pop store heists. An all-night spree of businesses after hours.

We enter the apartment. Two kids in a playpen. One in diapers. His lovely wife screams.

"You, you said this would never ever happen again." She buries her face in her hands, trembling.

"You need the money, Honey," he says. "We need it."

Poor thing crying at her wits end. She motions for me to sit on the couch, hands me a cup of coffee, trembling. Not sure if she was afraid or felt sorry for me. Maybe we both felt like chumps. I am ready to make my move.

Frank hauls the rest of the booty into the apartment. He and his wife argue, I bump him, strip my keys out of his hand and split. A pounding headache. Never been wasted like this before. Aha, the bastard spiked my drinks with pills. He is or was married. I am the patsy. My car was the getaway. Yikes.

I drive slowly to my brother Gene's place. Was I an accessory to a crime? I arrive mid-morning. Gene greeted me in his driveway and took in my story with studied intensity, and told me to stay put.

Unfamiliar with legal terminology, I considered my actions. Now I understand that an accessory before the fact aids, abets, assists, incites, or encourages the commission of a crime. I did none of that. But I was there. Did I know or voluntarily participate? No, I did not plan this. Was I an accessory after the fact? I did not shelter, relieve, or assist the felon after the crime. But I did not report it, either. That is bad but what about Frank and his family? I am the fall guy.

Gene comes back outside. "Your car is hot, put it in the garage till things cool down with the police for a few days. We're going to Tijuana for the weekend to see a bullfight."

My mood brightened. Maybe I will get through this.

Bullfights in Mexico were not controversial in the late 1960's. It was a new experience riding across the border to see a proud national pastime. We passed through Tijuana and headed west to the seaside Plaza Monumental. My self-loathing as patsy abated with the pageantry and spectacle of a sport brought to

Mexico by conquistadores over five hundred years ago. The complex could hold 20,000 people for the Sunday carnage. After lance men on padded horses pay tribute to dignitaries, banderillos throw darts at the bull to incite the action. With grace and style, the caped matador studied the bull's movement, and provoked further acts of incitement with determination. This is about life, death, fear, and fortitude.

My brother noticed my discomfort when the magnificent 2000-pound bull is killed. "Jim, they feed the poor people with the meat."

I feel oneness with the bull, we are chumps in games we did not design. I feel bad for Frank's wife and the business owners that were ripped off. When I returned to work on Monday, Frank was a no show. What a relief. He must have been apprehended or figured I would confront him. I was ambivalent about the knife and left it in my glove box.

Fifty years later I know this vintage knife was made by the oldest known knife manufacturer in the USA—Camillus Cutlery of New York. Craftsmanship and a special process since 1876 for making blades hard and sharp. The company branded its own knives and made them for other companies until going bankrupt in 2007.

Why do I still have this in possession after downsizing so many times? I never use it. Worth only thirty bucks to a collector. Yet this memento toggles time. When recently discovered among detritus of forgotten things, I am transported to 1968. Eighteen again, yet vintage too. I remember so much now. That wild summer of freedom and errors in judgment.

I drove that Plymouth coupe back to New England on a southern route through the mountains, the southwestern desert, to West Texas. The engine overheated and a retired, rawboned, rancher put me up for a couple days, ordered parts and fixed me up. The kindness of the man and his family reminded me of my parents. He shared wistful recollections of lost youth and respected me as a fellow traveler. Things are different today; I doubt my eighteen-year-old grandson's generation is interested in old men's stories or wisdom tales.

On the solo drive back to New England, I got weary trying to make time and nodded off. Hit the tapered side of a cement bridge abutment in Cincinnati. The front right side of my coupe flipped up and I pulled left without incident. Amazing how an autonomic response fired with adrenaline rush can save your life. Risky choices may be true origins of an irregular heartbeat.

My parents hardly recognized me with such shaggy hair, railroad cap, cutoff jeans, and sandals. Mom resisted the urge to question me much. Kodak Instamatic photos told the story of places I had been and getting to know my brother who had left home when I was eight. He and his family were good to me.

No one wants to be a pawn, patsy, or dupe. Hence a life-long quest for discernment, to observe character, and become a joyful skeptic inspired by a summer of lost youth. Trust but verify. Memento mori — "Remember, for tomorrow we must die."

Wandering From the Wanderer
Last Big U.S. Slave Ship

Nick Kalvin MD

Wanderer, a large sloop a year after launch in 1858, was bought at a New York City dock by William Corrie from Charleston. Then secretly, re-fitted with a hidden second deck. It departed New York City on June 18th. Official destination: Charleston. Instead, it sailed to the mouth of the Congo River. Stopped there September 16th. A month later, it departed for America.

November 1858, the Wanderer dropped sail and anchored just off Jekyll Island, Georgia loaded with the last large batch of slaves, 400 West African souls. Later, a smaller ship, Clotilda delivered a mere 110. Both shipments were clearly illegal, as Congress had outlawed importing slaves in 1807.

During Wanderer's voyage to US shores, Kwashi and Ibo, his leg-chain neighbor in the hull, managed to pry a rusty iron nail from a bottom beam of the stinking second deck. Wood around it had weakened with constant soaking of urine-sewage fouled water. Almost daily, someone died. Sick at both ends.

When a death occurred, crew members with rags over mouths and noses climbed down among the cargo. They unchained the body, tied a rope to ankles as relatives and friends wailed. Deckhands hoisted each corpse up and out. Tossed it to the sharks.

At sea, most days captives were taken topside in small groups. Bucket washed, sun-dried, fed and watered. Ibo and Kwashi repeatedly saw how leg-shackles opened with a metal stick. Their nail with some jiggling, could do the same.

During the night of November 28, 1858, off South Jekyll Isle, Georgia in Wanderer's secret compartment, Kwashi awoke. Strange, the ship so still. Slave auction soon. Above, he heard shouts, a heavy metal rumbling and a huge splash. Then all went quiet. He assumed that all aboard slept. All but him. Through the hold's hatch-vents, he saw the moon.

He nudged Ibo awake. With a hand over his friend's mouth, he urged Ibo to be silent. Whispering, they decided this was their last chance. Stealthily, Kwashi first unlocked the shackles around his ankles, then his friend's. Kwashi stowed the useful nail in his cheek. The pair tip-toed over sleepers. Crept up the ladder to the deck. Hearing nothing, they emerged. Went to the rail.

They were alone. In the moonlight, they saw land off the bow. Naked, they climbed down the anchor chain into cold salt water. Sores from shackles and whips stung. For silence, they swam without breaking surface. But that shoreline and trees, which looked deceptively close from the deck, suddenly seemed far away. After putting some distance between them and the ship, the boys began to swim more vigorously, attacking the waves with cupped hands and kicks, even as they knew the splashes might attract sharks lurking below. They had no idea where they were. Anyplace was better than the Wanderer.

Ibo, younger, not as good a swimmer as Kwashi, began to weaken. At times, dipping below the surface, bobbing back up to resume swimming. Kwashi slowed his pace to stay next to Ibo. Coughing water, Ibo said, "Kwashi, I'm tired." He quit paddling and began to sink. Frantically, Kwashi called out to him. He dove under the waves, reaching about for his friend. Finally, he felt something. Hair! He grabbed it. He heaved hard and pulled Ibo's face out of the water. "Friend, friend, don't die on me! Don't give up! Not now, after all this!"

Ibo spit water and clung to Kwashi, gasping for air. Staying close together, they slowly continued toward the mysterious land. Might it bring freedom, or death? What choice did they have but to try? Kwashi saw two dark pointed fins approaching through breaking waves as they neared the beach. He tried to touch the bottom, but it was still too deep to stand. Sharks are picking up the scent of our open wounds. The fins came closer. The larger shark suddenly brushed past Kwashi. Abrasive, rough hide of a lateral fin scratched his chest. His heart pounded in his ears, even over sound of the surf. "Ibo," he yelled, "Sharks!"

Dazed Ibo abruptly came alert, flooded with adrenaline. He desperately grabbed Kwashi's shoulders, his eyes wide as he scanned the water. Kwashi swam for both. Finally feeling bottom, Kwashi gratefully dug one foot after another into the sand, making it to the shallows. As he dragged his weaker-legged friend onto the beach, he watched the sharks turn back into deeper water.

Arms linked, panting, the boys flopped onto wet sand. Their teeth chattered, and their bodies shook from fright and cold. Sitting up, catching his breath, Kwashi looked about. Startled, he saw an older White man with a fringe of hair around his head, dressed in ragged dark brown robes cinched with a rope, kneeling on a sand dune. He was watching the ship.

The man turned and looked at Kwashi, almost as if he had been expecting him. He placed a left finger to his lips, as his right hand held up a metal cross, reflecting the moonlight. Then he stood, beckoning slowly to follow as he walked backwards into the woods.

Kwashi and Ibo exchanged glances. They should have been afraid of this White, but mysteriously, they weren't. They nodded. Ibo whispered, "Seems like it's time to trust a white man." Silently, the boys got up and followed him. After a long walk through thick brush and vines, they came upon a thatch-roof hut. They followed the man inside. A big, husky, bearded Black greeted them in Igbo, their native tongue. Blankets were handed to the shivering arrivals. The big Black spoke with a deep, but gentle voice. "I and the religion man will not harm you. Indeed, we were sent here to help slaves escape."

The big Black identified himself as Jesus, alternating from Igbo to Spanish with the elder fringe-top man whom he said was Friar José. During bilingual discussions, Kwashi and Ibo gratefully spooned bowls of hot gruel with bacon rind, sitting beside a small fire on the dirt floor.

"On the next night, you cross swampy lowlands until you

reach a tiny dock. End of this Isle. Christians and freed men will row you two islands north before sunrise. On the second one, you will hide in mangrove swamps by day. At full dark, follow Big Dipper's North Star to a pointed, a rocky shore, marked by five broken tree stumps and a waist high boulder with a cross scratched into the sea-facing side. Hide behind that rock. Our people will come, waving a metal cross. Take you by boat, to a white stone cottage with a red door, on the mainland. All our helpers along your way will first show a simple metal cross, just like that of Friar José. All are Christians who risk arrest and prison to end slavery."

Friar José and Black Jesus described a long trek. "Many stops. Many guides. More red doors. Some have small, black-man statues with a ribbon on one arm. If green, rap the code. You will get shelter, provisions until the next leg."

Friar José emptied two burlap sacks. Each held trousers, belt, three shirts, stockings boots, a block of gritty, tar-smelling soap, sandals, tin bowl, plate and cup, several rags, string, fire-flint, short wool coat, knife, spoon, fork, straw hat. He showed the boys how to dress, then how to use the fire-flint. Kwashi found his boots were too tight. More so wearing socks.

Seeing that, the Holy Man rummaged through other pre-pared sacks. Found donated boots which fit. He traded the boots with Kwashi, commenting, "Sandals won't do for the entire trip as you will discover."

Black Jesus explained what the soap blocks were for. Dis-cussed customs, dress, nudity, behavior expected of them. The boys' eyebrows raised at prescribed gentle treatment of females, rules for latrines, also called "necessary houses" and chamber pots.

"Most important," said Black Jesus, "be deathly quiet, stay hidden during travel, unless told otherwise by members of the Underground Railway. Escape will take months. You'll finally come to a huge river, named the Ohio. Once across, you will be safe. Important you learn language on your way."

Exhausted by the escape, sharks, a long swim, excitement, duplicate lectures, bellies filled with decent hot food, the escapees fell into a deep sleep just before dawn. Remained so until sunset. Upon awakening, they ate dark bread, cheese, drank water and dressed, Black Jesus tested them. "Now, repeat my instructions. Pay attention. You cannot afford carelessness nor mistakes."

They recited everything word for word. As the two slaves stepped out into the night, with travel sacks over their shoulders, Black Jesus and Friar José hugged them and prayed over them. They both pointed out the North Star, then went back into the hut.

Fearful but hopeful, Kwashi and Ibo began to walk toward the star into the swamp.

They found the white stone cottage with the red door near Brunswick, Georgia. The journey overland began with a two-mule cart for five days, just to reach a rural sawmill, west of Savannah. When it rained, water trickled down through a cavity soaking the boys silently hidden under a load of logs. Their place to stay, from dawn to dark.

They spoke to each other only in soft whispers. Early on the trek, they heard strange voices, people inspecting, prodding the load. Searching for runaway slaves. Kwashi and Ibo held their breath and prayed as Friar José had taught them. At safe stops, Underground guides used a series of taps to let the boys out. Kwashi and Ibo could squeeze out or get back in, by moving some of the cart bottom center, nail-free slats further apart. During stops with strange voices and no coded tapping, they avoided making any noise, breathing shallow and soundless. No movement or shifting positions in the cramped space until the trip safely resumed. Sometimes the young men feared that the thudding sounds of their hearts were certain to expose them.

The next cart carried square-cut timbers, as they continued towards a river village north of Augusta where they were transferred to another cart. Next time they hid under cotton bales piled aboard an up-river barge. Kwashi and Ibo had room to sit, but not lay down. They silently dealt with a slop bucket, bottled water, crackers, atop a solid deck for two days. In a cold rain, the barge docked. Offloaded after dark, Kwashi and Ibo were quickly ushered to a safe house nearby where they washed, ate and collapsed on a real bed. Then, more cart-caves. Weeks beneath different loads: sacked corn, produce, wood, barrels of syrup, whiskey, grain. They relished the few sheltering homes, barns or an occasional church, where they washed and changed clothes, enjoyed hot food. At each stop, they were taught more English.

During the second half of the journey, they mostly walked silently during darkness with no lanterns, rain or not. To avoid roads and towns, the Underground folk took them through woodlands, over steep hills and through thorny fields. By day, they rested. Speaking with and learning from their rescuers in a hide-out was a treat. A South Carolina dentist showed them how he safely removed rotten, painful teeth. Also, how to let fluid out of blisters on their feet without removing the skin, for faster healing. He gave them a bottle of pine-sap skin toughener. At the next stop, a host family showed them on a map, how far they had come and how much farther they needed to go. It seemed the trip would never end. It was difficult to keep spirits up, but the host families encouraged and prayed with them. Reminded them that if they left the Underground, they'd likely be caught, whipped, returned South in a less hospitable manner, for a cash reward.

A huge, snowfall in the mountains of North Carolina detained them. Closed the roads for two weeks. The farmer used that extra time to teach his traveling guests. He taught: Leather-craft, cobbling, boot/shoe repair, how to dig root cellars, care of horses and mules, reshoeing them, doing harness repair, wood working, and making glues to repair carpentry. While they eagerly learned, they polished their improving English with the farmer and his family.

At night, the Missus and three children read aloud from a Bible by the stove or fireplace. The family, Kwashi and Ibo ended every session with a 1779 hymn. A favorite of the Missus, Amazing Grace, written by a remorseful former slaver captain, John Newton.

When snow depth allowed departure, the farmer and wife gave Kwashi and Ibo Bibles, hand-carved walnut wood bead crucifix necklaces, kits of leather-goods tools for their burlap bags, warmer coats made from two-layered wool horse blankets. Behind the barn, he introduced them to a pair of friends. These were guides for the next steps to Freedom.

After another month of travel Northwest, one morning, the railway folks introduced Kwashi and Ibo to twenty-six other slaves, already gathered in a North Kentucky church atop a hill on the south side of the mighty Ohio River. They had escaped from several plantations. Some had been in captivity for decades. Came by dozens of different Underground routes.

A few could read and write. One man, Jasper, who figured he was thirty-five years old, had been sold off a slave ship in New Orleans when he was only twelve. Jasper also complained of pain. He had a back tooth with a deep cavity. Kwashi and Ibo were able to remove it after explaining they had been shown how to do it by a dentist in North Georgia.

The Underground members watched attentively and applauded when Ibo raised the offending tooth as Kwashi inserted a wad of boiled cloth for Jasper to bite on at the empty socket for a time, to stop the bleeding.

A night later, the weather turned colder with more snow. After a church supper and Bible reading, the minister called Jasper up before the altar. The cleric cleared his throat and put an arm around Jasper's shoulders, "Gentlemen, I am going to have Jasper read to you. He assures me he can do it, despite some recent dentistry." Jasper smiled, proudly showing off the new vacancy in his mouth. The preacher reached under the lectern, pulled out a book. He held it up.

"This story was written by a white lady, Harriet Beecher Stowe. She lived almost twenty years in Cincinnati, Ohio, not far away from where we are. This was published in early 1850. The book's name is Uncle Tom's Cabin. It became very popular. It greatly increased dislike of slavery here in the United States, probably more than any other influence. More importantly, it convinced many people to help those of us already in the Underground," tapping a finger on the book.

"We received money, goods, clothing, shoes, lines of communication plus hundreds of volunteers. Even in the deepest South. This has allowed us to do even more in the cause of freedom of all races. Tomorrow night, we will take you to a ferry boat. Get you across the Ohio to Cincinnati. There, we will split into groups of four. You can choose the groups yourselves to keep friends or relations together. Each group will go a different village or city in Ohio where you can work, live as free men. Even start a family. Or move away. Each group will have a local railway agent living there who will help you get settled. They'll give advice or aid when you need some." He opened the novel to the ribbon marker. Handed it to Jasper. "If you will, please begin the first Chapter."

Jasper's reading moved everybody in the church. There were tears, and many smiles of gratefulness. Afterward, Kwashi and Ibo put on their long, high collared, horse-blanket coats and gloves. They went out to the side door and walked to the north end of the church's hilltop graveyard among the snowcapped tombstones. They had taken to smoking at night before bed. They lit corncob pipes. Through clouds of Virginia tobacco's fragrance and mists of breath, they looked down and out. They could see across the huge Ohio River valley. Gazing at the spread-out lights of Cincinnati on the other side of the river, the men leaned into each other. Touched heads. Ibo whispered, "There it is, brave-friend-who-saved-me, the Promised Land at last. At times I doubted we would ever get here."

Kwashi kissed the forehead of his companion. "As did I. Ibo, if the sharks had grabbed you, I would have certainly died, fighting or drowning trying to save you." With snowflakes gathering on their dark hair, they joined hands to say a prayer for their tribe members left behind on the Wanderer.

REMARKS: Before written history, for 4,000 years or more, warring Black tribes and empires indentured or enslaved losing tribes. They marched slave caravans via Sahara Desert routes to Carthage, Rome and other powers. After 732 A.D., Islam spread across North Africa, then down and into each coast. Believers expanded, accelerated the rate of blacks sold to a rapidly growing, labor hungry Caliphate. More caravans were added to West Coast Mali and Ghana, Zanzibar on the East Coast. One research estimation, 17 million. A vigorous enterprise, spurred by the warning, "Convert to Islam, get us slaves or become a slave."

In 1650, Brazil was the first Western Hemisphere power to engage in the slave trade. African slave dealers were astonished when the Brazilian ship refused to accept the cargo. Ship's physician had examined the offering. He told his Captain that all males were freshly castrated. The Black Islamist slavers protested, "Sire, this has long been the way for the Caliphate. Majority young females meant for sex slaves or harems, one-fifth or tenth castrated males for service and guards." The Brazilian Captain replied, "That may be, but our gold, our goods stay aboard. We demand the majority be uncastrated, healthy young males. A lesser number, young females fit to breed once across the Big Water. No sale unless you comply. We go back aboard to wait." With that first encounter Brazil's Captain turned the thousand-year, Fundamental Islam-African slave trade model upside down.

Marryin' A. Suffragette
In Florida Woods, 1914

Nick Kalvin MD

My life changed when I saw a girl who could stop a clock. At least my heart did for a few seconds. Somehow, I kept on strolling down Broadway Street, after Willis went over to the 4-H tent.

By golly, closer I got, the better she looked! Standing behind a curb-side table. Wearing a Suffragette's white dress with yellow ribbons. An outfit full of a body what likely broke the mold. From center road, I admired Island-girl's honey-colored skin, and dark curly hair. Above her table, hand-painted letters on a banner hanging on twine 'twixt two poles:

JORDAN RIVER BAPTIST CHURCH BUILDING FUND
Sweet Potato Pie Three Cents A Slice

Trying not to fly over like some dang nail to a magnet, I ambled over slow. Saw on her ample bosom, a name tag, "Janeeza." It was tough not to stare. She fixed on me with beautiful Morning-Glory blue eyes. Something which happens in mixed-race folk, even green. My mouth felt dry. Watching her, stupid me bumped the table.

She spoke first, "Hello, sir. I guess you want some pie."

Working to put words out, "Yes, miss, fear I'd be regretful, if I never got a taste."

I pointed up at her sign, "I'll pay more, cause of the church. I'm Jeffry Wilson, from Lee County. Visiting Cousin Willis Barton. He's over at the 4-H tent. Wants a new milkin goat for Auntie Bess."

She laughed, showing off pouty, natural cherry lips and pearly teeth. "I know the Bartons, Mister Wilson. Welcome to Fellsmere. I'm Janeeza Folsom. Nice to meet you. Now, let's fetch your pie." She scanned the lot. Picked one from under her cheesecloth fly cover. Sliced a piece.

Dang, she's cut almost a fourth!

I held out my left palm with two nickels. "If you please, call me, Jeff."

Honey-colored fingers reached for the coins. When she touched my palm, a tingle ran up my arm. It made both armpits sweaty. My cheeks got hot. Seemed she was amused by my discomfort. Or maybe, I hoped, liked what she was seeing.

"Never had this kinda pie, Miss Folsom."

She handed me that huge slice atop a tin plate. I took it. Our skins touched the second time. Another tingle. This time, right side. Acting calm and polite, I bit off the corner, smelled nice spices. The sweet pie melted in my mouth.

"Oh, Miss Folsom, it's wonderful! You'll sell out before this ado is done."

This time, it was her blushing, "I'm so happy you like it. Happens, I baked this one myself. Just call me, Janeeza."

"What could beat tastin your pie an' makin you happy?"

She smiled those kissy lips. "That's the way things should go. Thank you for the extra money."

Picturing her hands working a roll of flour dough, I took a second bite. Looked up and down Broadway Street, only sizable one so far. No church. Just a general store, tiny post office, scattered houses, sewing-knitting shop, tobacco stand, a busy tavern, and a feed barn. All with vacant lots between. "By the way, where's the church?"

"Out yonder," she pointed to a cluster of pines. "Out there. In them woods. An open-side old Army tent with split-log benches. We meet twice a week."

"Why out in the woods?" I got back to my pie.

Janeeza laughed, "Now, Jeff, where you think Adam and Eve first talked with God? Silly, happens that's where Jordan River property is."

I felt the fool. Handed back her tin plate. Shrugged. "Guess folks always prayed everywhere, for most anythin'."

Getting calmer, I chuckled. "Why not them woods? I mean, what's better than outdoor song and prayer? Tell me all about your church."

While Pie Goddess gathered her thoughts, I straightened up. Thankful, I'd bathed. Wore new denim shirt, coveralls, best boots for the trip to town. Even combed my blond hair with pomade. Looked clean, if not pleasing.

Her voice, somehow seemed far off, so I leaned closer to hear. Caught a whiff of lavender. Pulled back a bit. Couldn't be caught sniffing at her like some mangy cur.

"After Reconstruction, an old slave holder here, who owned 640 acres, wrote a new will. In it he left sixty-four acres, to his eight former slaves or their kids and grandkids. One slave, my Grand Pap, Ezekiel Folsom, was among the listed.

"Well, that slave owner took ill, passed. Soon after his son and three daughters tried to get the slave part of his will took out. Claimed, due to advanced age, the gift was a clear sign of mental problems. After that, legal wranglin' went on for years. Lawyers for sons and daughters, then, their kids, kept filin' objections. Lucky, we had Christian lawyers. Good ones. Helped us free. One discovered a couple letters penned by the slave owner to friends, prior to date of his will change. His own handwritin told how, beset by sin and regret, he desired to leave his apology, as a gift to his one-time slaves, when he died. One might think that ended things in 1900.

"When those letters came out, slave owner's kin then switched tactic. Said, since that change required a church be built, and Darkies named, never put one up, they didn't deserve any land, anyhow."

I defended her take, "Gosh, Janeeza, who'd build on land not owned?"

Janeeza sighed. "Exactly! Even former slaves, their children didn't see need until they had the whole property outright. Finally, things settled. Last judge pointed out that the family inheritors accepted the rest of that Will in good faith. Now, obliged to release the 64-acre gift to us. Judge gave us the deed, free and clear. He ordered the court clerk to draw up official family trees. Such to become part of deed documents, from the original eight slaves named in the will, seven males and one female, down to present time."

She laughed. "Weekend after, we got out to the land. Already surveyed. Marked off at least twice, during courthouse spats. Friends, neighbors, Colored, White, Indian, all kinda folks who favored a church, showed up with tools, horses, oxen. We cleared two acres in the center for the church site and a cemetery.

"Used cut logs for benches, boards for the altar, choir stand once we set a floor of smoothed oak planks, raised up a foot from dirt. It's pretty among the scrub oak, cypress, Spanish-moss and pines. Then we put that used Army tent over top, in case of rain. We had a big cook-out at day's end. Now, gatherin' money for a permanent church.

"Meantime, my family, kin branched from other seven slaves, built cabins or plan to do so, on one-acre parcels of outlyin' land. But Jordan River BC still has four plus acres next to it. Some say, best saved for a Christian school."

She tipped her head. Smiled. "Well, that's my church story."

"Janeeza, it's one to inspire generations."

Gazing at her that minute, I had to wonder.

How was it, I ended up by this table, this Friday night, while she worked there? Why, a cousin family here in Indian River County, nor' east of Lake Okeechobee and Lee County? Why Dad, Scotch-English came to the US? Married a girl from Germany? Why his crops and yearlings all sold so quick, and for a great price, provided me time-off to visit?

Still pondering, I said to her, "I'm glad Will insisted we come downtown, Janeeza. Seems he knows most everyone. The new Mayor we met, said over 250-300 people live here with more comin' each year. Told me this place will soon be a legal town, Fellsmere. Named after the biggest citrus farm here about."

Janeeza nodded. "All correct, Jeff. Say, half hour, my shift is over. I'll be free. There's a brass band, set up to play inspiring music in the park. Lots going on, for a bitty place, so far south of the Mason-Dixon."

She looked down. Fussed with the already straight cheese-cloth covering the pies. "Would you like to go . . . with me?"

My heart flipped again. "Yes, Janeeza, I would enjoy hearin' that band. More so, with you. Let me go tell Willis where I'll be. Then, come back. Help you until the next pie seller comes."

Later, sitting shoulder-to-shoulder on folding chairs, we enjoyed patriotic songs, hymns going back to the fight against England, right up through the Civil War. We clapped and yelled after each. It was heavenly, her so close to me. I thought of hand-holding. Decided not be so quick. Was taken aback when she tapped the beat on my wrist with Yankee Doodle and Onward Christian Soldiers at the end.

After the concert, by moonlight I walked her out to her

cabin. Willis had the good sense not to show up. Just went back to the farm with a new goat.

Later that night, at Will's, I penned a letter home. Asked permission to stay 'til just before Christmas. Sunday morn I went out to a raggedy Army tent church. She was in the choir. Looked pleased, seeing me. Folks of all colors were there. Pine sap aroma filled the air. I got goosebumps when she sang a solo. After service Janeeza introduced me to her parents and the pastor.

They were very welcoming. Her Ma invited me for Sunday dinner. Their home was recent built. Nice, large, one-story log cabin with a surrounding screen porch. Not near as big as my family's two-story wood-frame. The Folsom cabin still smelled like fresh wood. Simple, cozy with a swing-out iron cookware, river-stone fireplace. Above it, a built-in oven. Her Ma was proudest of a water pump inside by the kitchen sink.

While we enjoyed tasty, stewed chicken with lots of sides, Janeeza asked, "Jeff, since you're not workin' would you help me fund raise?"

With her folks awaiting my words, I acted like I needed to think, before saying,' "Be happy to."

So, begun my regular twice a week church attendance. I became good friends with Rev. Farnsworth. The following week-end Janeeza, hands-on-hips proud, showed me her library. Was in a back hallway of their home. Two bookcases made of planks and bricks. Over them, hung copies of the Declaration, Constitution, Bill of Rights, and a magazine picture of the signers.

She smiled, "Jeff, feel free to make use, whenever you want."

Over some weeks, I did. Her books included two medical ones. With pictures! She had stacks of boxed stuff, clipping, letters, pamphlets. All arranged by alphabet-lettered cardboard pieces. I even come across a pink paper booklet, Avoiding Pregnancy. Those pine planks held stuff what would raise eyebrows back in Fort Myers.

She took me to one Suffragette meeting. I felt odd, the only male. Membership included wealthy local white ladies, who paid uncommon respect to colored girls. The lot was excited. Talked about Fellsmere's ladies going to be first to vote in the US, that is, after Wyoming. They wanted marriage law changes, too. Said The Declaration included females as to those enabled rights, not just men.

Two ladies were in The National Women's Party. One picketed the White House. She read from a newspaper column:

"Marriage, under current religion and law, is legal prostitution. Makes wives creatures of economic necessity, under control of provider husbands. Brides become naught but cooks, cleaners, diaper changers. Obliged to meet male needs whenever, however the gent demands. Never mind, her wants, mood, plans or state of health."

I tasted acid, hearing this. That writer's take on marriage didn't fit married folks I knew, including my parents. Course, they never discussed private doings. I pushed my chair back a bit. It squeaked. Ladies turned. Looked at the only man.

Another hefty white lady in a big hat, sporting Egret plumes, said, "Sir, today, many women consider marriage to be a cruel one-sided arrangement, which ages them quickly due to sequential pregnancies and miscarries. An early grave, alas, the only rest or escape."

Gosh, seemed like she blamed me for this Devil's kettle of problems. I did agree, folks shouldn't marry too early, of whatever sex.

A bit hot, I spoke. First and last time. "Ladies, all I know is what I seen in my family and amongst friends, relatives and neighbors. Most marriages seem, at least, alright."

Janeeza answered when no one else did, "Yes, Jeff. But truth is, some are horrible. In cases like these worn-to-death teenage women, the supposed grievin widowers are all too quick to re-marry. Get younger teen gals to carry on. Wear out another. Maybe more."

The group bobbed heads. One lady teared up. Recalled a recent case. More nodding and tsking.

Thank heavens, that meeting ended, 'cause I was one sweaty mess.

Friday nights on Broadway Street, I watched Janeeza orate. She stood atop a big citrus crate. Mostly, a dozen walkers stopped to listen. More walked by. Some sour faced.

"Women, too, have a right to work," she loudly claimed. "They have a right to education. To become doctors, lawyers, teachers, run a business, be writers, inventors, scientists. At very least, they should finish school before parents marry them off too early, like thirteen or fourteen."

She looked excited, flushed. Wonderful. Even in a simple strap-top dress I watched her sew the week before from dyed flour sacks. A nice white sweater-shawl covered her shoulders. Little black curls bounced around that angel face as she waved her hands, making points. She looked each person direct in the eye when answering questions. I was so proud of her, I could've burst. After her talk and some jawin' with her ladies, I walked her back home, carried her crate platform.

On the way, I asked, "Janeeza, aren't you, your friends ever scared of folks who disagree?"

"Jeff, they have a right to disagree. Me, my ladies, we don't seek trouble. We jus don't think that what's always been, should always keep on as was. We want females to have a say, when it comes to love. It won't make women harlots. Jus means we're allowed to use our own minds as to romance."

Her creamy honey-colored skin seemed to redden. She looked away, before going on. "So, females can take a first little step, should they see fit, like men. Take me for example. I never been with a man. Never felt the need. Nor, for a child. Honest, til recent, never considered either."

My heart flipped. I almost dropped her crate. Near fell out with a bad case of the vapors out on the dirt road. Next step, clearly up to me. But, beset by jitters I could only say goodnight at her front porch. Still fearful her speeches might cause trouble or even get her lynched.

She got lucky. The Women's Christian Temperance Union and Anti-Saloon League sided with local Suffragettes. All said cash pay envelopes, that should feed and house a family, too often got spent on drink, or other women. Caused spats over money gone. Then drunk sex. Mayhap, another babe begun when sots staggered home.

The idea that single females could "play the field," was thought to be sinful, uppity sass. Suffragettes were called "Free lovers" and "Varietists" by newspapers. Worse on the street. Re-ligious leaders in parts of Florida predicted trouble. Whatever, big change was afoot.

It was plain, I had to abide the change, or lose Janeeza.

A week later, time neared for me to start home. We were walking back to her place, from a speech. By her front porch, she looked at me. Unusually quiet. I knew it was now or never.

"Please, come back with me," I said, "Meet my family." I moved closer, savored her sweet breath, kissed her gently.

Whispered in her ear. "Please, marry me, Janeeza. I never felt this way afore, but it sure seems like love."

I feared she'd be upset or worse. Instead, I was flabbergasted when she put her arms around my neck. Kissed me. A long, long kiss.

She pulled back, fixed eyes on me. Then, she counted on lovely fingers, stuff she felt need to say:

"Rule one, your folks accept me. Chance be, your folks won't be comfy, face to face. Me, a Quadroon. A one-fourth Darkie on your arm!

"Two, we meet your neighbors, school pals. Probably, your letters didn't get shared much, specially 'bout a Negro woman in your life.

"Three, if we marry, we go in as equals. In everythin'. The kitchen. Buyin' stuff. Payin' bills. Religion. Havin' children or not. Makin' sex or not."

I started to agree, but she put a warm hand to my mouth.

Clearly, she wasn't done. "Rule Four, if, and when we church-marry, 'in them woods,' instead of dusty vows, we swear our love. Pledge to live it full steam."

I couldn't help but smile.

"Five, both sign legal paper allowin' either to walk away, should need arise. Rule six, I get to work outside the house, stay in the Movement."

She stopped, looked at me. Started to raise a hand to her mouth, then lowered it. Like she feared she'd blabbed too long, about too much. But that needful fire, courage, strength was her nature.

I took her shoulders, "Miss Janeeza Folsom, it was one ox-wagon load of rules and words you dumped on me, when a simple 'yes' would suffice. But bein' a modern, equality-drove man, I agree to each. You are special. I know Ma and Pa, Sisters Leslie and Louanne will love you too. But I need to hear you say the words. So, will you marry me?"

She hugged me tight. Was like Heaven. Her pressed against me. She smiled. Smoothed my shirt collar. "Jeffie, yes. Yes, I freely choose to become your wife."

She kissed my nose. Finger-brushed my hair. "Come in

for coffee. My folks are still up. Let's tell them. They say you're a genuine man, not just another hot-pants stud hangin round. Mister Jeffry Wilson, I love you. So much, it aches."

She looked puzzled. "Now, how can that be?"

"Must be natural, as I feel the same."

Ten years later, we have four great kids of varied shade, going to Jordan River BC School. My folks and hers love each one so. Cousin Willis and I bought a farm. dairy and citrus. Now planting some imported trees, Mango, and Avocado.

Living up to Rule Four, Janeeza and I still are like honeymooners when alone. Each night I thank the Lord for putting us together. No question, Lord Jesus and Janeeza made me a better man.

She's campaigning again. This time, Indian River County District seat. Done all she can at City Council. So, she'll be busy as usual. Guess that's the way Janeeza will always be. And I'm so proud she is.

I Promise, LeRoy

Michael M. Meguid M.D.

I caught up with my residents as they hurriedly pushed the gurney with a combative young man into the OR. As I was the surgeon on call, all they told me over the phone, shortly after 4 a.m., was that an eighteen-year-old man had slipped off a third-floor window ledge while trying to break into an apartment some thirty minutes earlier. He was in profound shock, running a low blood pressure from a presumed life-threatening internal hemorrhage. They'd meet me in the OR. Within minutes I was speeding down the Mass Pike to Boston City Hospital, fueled by an adrenaline rush.

As with such blunt abdominal cases where major internal bleeding is suspected, few invasive or radiological tests had been done. The one quick, on-the-spot test my residents did in the ER—the semi-quantitative newsprint test—was positive. In this test, a needle attached to IV tubing and 500ml of saline is stuck into the lower abdominal midline. The entire volume is rapidly run into the abdominal cavity, and then the bag is lowered so that the saline siphons back into the plastic bag. If the return-fluid is sufficiently turbid with blood so that newsprint cannot be read through it, research shows that the results highly correlate with bleeding from a major internal organ such as the liver. The key is to get the patient to the OR as quickly as possible, open up the abdomen, and take care of the injury to stop the hemorrhage before the patient bleeds to death.

LeRoy lay naked on the gurney, and I saw with envy that he had a fine ebony physique; in contrast, my body older showed the signs of physical neglect. He was very muscular, with a thick neck from lifting weights, and well-developed shoulders and arms. He had the classic six-pack abdomen. He had obviously spent much time body building. I wished I had such a body; instead, I'd spent my time building my mind. Several large-bore IVs had been stuck into his arms and were wide open, as fluids poured into his veins trying to keep pace with his bleeding, supporting his low blood pressure. The Foley catheter in his bladder drained cloudy yellow urine, of blood, and suggestive an injury to his kidneys. His youthful body shimmered in the OR light. His belly was distended.

He was inadequately sedated, thrashing and restless, fighting his endotracheal tube which was providing 100% oxygen to his lungs. He tugged at his restrained arms. Our eyes met—a wild and frightened stare. Reading his mind, I too wondered if he'd make it. Abruptly, his head and arms slumped as the anesthetist gave him a slug of a sedative. As we cautiously moved him onto the OR table, I saw that he had a grossly disfigured, twisted, left thigh bone from a fractured femur. He was bleeding into his thigh, which was tense and double its usual size, shining with a bluish hue from accumulated blood.

Without scrubbing, I gowned and gloved. The circulating nurse poured a bottle of antiseptic Betadine over his abdomen, which ran down the sides of his belly and dripped onto the floor. She secured the "seat belt" over his good right leg and cradled his fractured leg in pillows. The orthopedic resident was on his way to see the fracture and the hastily obtained ER x-ray of his twisted leg, while the anesthetist was fretting about his continued low blood pressure, egging me on and calling out for more units of blood. Together with my resident, we rapidly draped his torso, the wet Betadine soaked through the waterproof drapes and the front of my gown, into my underpants stinging my balls, and dripping into my shoes. We worked feverishly against time.

Shortly before 5 a.m., I hesitated for a very brief moment, scalpel in hand, reluctant to place a scar through his beautiful abdominal wall. Then I made a single, swift, full thickness midline incision through his hairless skin—one bold slash with the knife into his abdominal cavity from xyphoid to pubis. Stem to stern, straight through his belly button.

I expected to find lots of free blood, a fractured liver or spleen, or ruptured vessels—usual injuries associated with a fall from a significant height.

I found . . . nothing!

Nada.

Nothing.

There was no free blood in his abdomen, and his organs

were all intact. LeRoy's shock was from the profuse bleeding into the muscles of his thigh, tracking up the retroperitoneal space at the back of his pelvis and up into his lower back, pushing the roots of his guts forward, where some blood seeped through from the back into the abdominal cavity. It was barely sufficient to have given a positive newsprint test. Could the intern in the ER have over-interpreted the degree of blood in the return?

The orthopedic attending, a colleague, trooped into the OR trailed by his entourage of residents and medical students.

"Well?"

"Nothing!"

"Really?"

"NO . . .thing."

I could only shake my head. Suspecting that I may have overlooked an injury, I systematically re-examined his entire abdomen: every single organ, his liver, spleen, stomach, pancreas, the small and large bowel, his major vessels, his kidneys and bladder, every organ between his diaphragm and his pelvic floor — at a more deliberate and measured pace, taking my time to be absolutely sure and positively certain that I was not overlooking a subtle injury.

Again, I found no internal injuries. "Nothing!"

Without question, the source of his bleeding was the broken femoral shaft bone, a very vascular structure. Suddenly I felt deflated and drained. The adrenaline rush drained out of me. But I was glad for LeRoy.

What had been a close call was over.

He was now going to live.

He was now going to make it.

LeRoy was going to recover.

He was now going able to go home.

At the same time, I felt remorseful that I had scarred his beautiful body with the standard trauma-type slash incision with the intention of saving his life.

After closing his belly, I scrubbed out while the orthopedic surgeon moved in to fix his fractured leg and stop the bleeding bone. Protocol dictated that LeRoy became their patient and he was transferred to the care of the orthopedic service as I and my exhausted team of residents bowed out.

By noon LeRoy, with a fixed left leg was been moved into

the ICU, where he lay in the first bed by the door.

***

During the next few weeks, I saw him at least twice a day as I passed his bed on my way through the ICU to see my patients during my early morning and late evening rounds.

One day, after thirty days his bed was empty.

"Where is LeRoy?"

"Dead," was the reply.

"LeRoy died?"

"Yes. This morning."

I was stunned. How could an 18-year-old physically fit human specimen just die from a broken leg? I went into the bowels of Boston City Hospital where medical records were kept to review his hospital records. These showed he had no signs of other injuries. Yet what they recorded was shockingly revealing.

***

On admission, LeRoy had weighed one hundred and eighty pounds. He lost almost thirt-four pounds during his thirty-day hospital stay. Although the physician's order was written for an oral diet, his record showed that he had eaten very little. No calorie counts had been ordered to record whether he ate or how much he consumed. In essence he had been maintained on an intravenous drip of 5% glucose in saline. One liter provides fifty grams of glucose, or barely two teaspoons of sugar—the equivalent of 170 calories. Every day he had received three liters, getting in total approximately six teaspoons of sugar—510 calories, or about two candy bars a day for thirty days.

To survive his massive leg injury plus the insult of the shock from the bleeding plus the stress of two major operations he would need at least 3000 calories per day to recover. Not just as glucose, but also as protein, fat, vitamins, trace elements, and minerals to permit healing of his injured tissues. In the absence of intense medical nutrition support, his muscles broke down to provide his daily nutrient needs. When he ran out of his critical muscle mass, he'd weakened his breathing muscles—the diaphragm and the intercostal muscles. Unable to get oxygen to sustain life, his lungs gave up and his heart stopped beating.

As I read LeRoy's medical and nurses notes, I saw his eyes staring at me, pleading to save him.

I had failed.

LeRoy died in a Boston hospital from a trauma induced hospital-related malnutrition! The date was August 1976. I decided this would never happen again on my watch. I picked up the phone and called the head of MIT's Human Nutrition Department. I was signed up to their graduate nutrition program.

So, at the age of 35, after three years of grammar school, five years of medical school, and seven years of surgical training, that included two research years, I sat once more with twenty-two-year-old super-smart kids in a classroom. I was draped over my desk exhausted from operating on emergencies during the previous night, going to classes at MIT in the morning, doing my elective operations at Boston City Hospital to earn a living in the afternoon, and often operating on emergencies at night. Many times, I felt bedraggled and sleep-deprived. Did I really want to do this? I felt like a misfit as various teachers — experts and geniuses — droned on and on and on about various topics of nutrition and biochemistry. My pager, akin to a live grenade, was dangling from my belt threatening to go off at any moment. I hoped and prayed that it wouldn't, so I could remain as inconspicuous as possible.

Thus, I lived the double life of a Professor of Surgery in Boston, on one side of the Charles River, and a humble, exhausted insecure graduate student on its other side in Cambridge. Over a three-year period, I acquired the useful nutrition knowledge which I needed and which I ultimately applied to my trauma and cancer patients — happy that I was honoring the promise I made to LeRoy.

* * *

Notes: A version of this story appeared in the Columbia Medical Review in 2014 and will appear in the author's forthcoming book Great Joys, Great Sorrows — Passion & Compassion Volume 4 of the quartet A Surgeon's Tale.

Nature Bound

Donna Kremer

I hope I'm not just considered ballast. Maybe Garrett values my photography skills. I don't want to know the reason. But I'm glad he's asking me even though it seems more natural that he would have asked his dad. Not wanting him to change his mind, I nonchalantly say "Sure," masking my enthusiasm.

"Be ready by six?" he asks.

I nod my head in assent. A smile pulls on my lips as I turn away. I get to go fishing with my son!

When I creep out of bed the next morning it's still dark and the quietness is thick with anticipation. At twenty-three years of age, Garrett has learned that getting up early has its merits, especially when it comes to fishing. He's already dressed. He moves about quietly with purpose, gathering his fly rods and equipment, while I pour hot coffee in a thermos. Not a word is spoken between us as we prepare for our adventure. Within minutes we carry our gear to his truck, secure it in the empty nooks, gently close the doors, and pull out into the cool, early dawn.

The silence between us is surprisingly comfortable. The heater fan and thrum of the tires on the concrete make the only sounds. Most people would say I have a firm grip on my chatting skills but here it's not necessary as the headlights skim over the lines in the road. I don't know where we're going but it doesn't matter. The expectancy of the day builds inside of me.

Although it may seem we have a solid relationship, I've always longed for acceptance from my son. I have played the role of indulgent mother, giving him many things to foster his happiness, like a dog bringing a bone to its master. I've driven thousands of miles over his lifetime as his personal chauffeur to school, library programs, swim lessons, play dates, soccer practice, drivers training, and late-night parties. Instead of engaging in lively conversation through the years, he invariably chose to sleep in the passenger's seat, closing me out.

It's not that Garrett is unkind or apathetic. In kindergarten, his teacher remarked that "Garrett is a favorite among his peers." Others called him the class clown. My best friends today say, "He is so funny!" Even his Instagram shows a face beaming with happiness. In my presence, though, he leaves me in silence. I wait patiently for him, anticipating chances to see the amiable person that others do.

When Garrett was a baby, we bought a tiny 1940s cottage on a local lake in Michigan where he learned to catch blue gill, jiggling a piece of corn at the end of a Mickey Mouse fishing pole. He soon upgraded to a spinning reel and eventually a fly rod. That lake was his training ground for the fishing he was soon to master around his new home at the University of Miami. There, he cast into the Atlantic, local ponds, and even ditches along the highways. His love for the sport has become obsessive and I am glad to have this opportunity to share in it.

We are the first to arrive at the boat launch and it feels good to have the place to ourselves. We unload the truck, transferring our belongings to Garrett's royal blue boat. Similar to a canoe, it has a wider base for stability and a flat stern equipped with a small motor. The emblem on the side says Gheenoe in script. Garrett reconditioned Grandma's portable bedside toilet into a raised platform in back. His practicality and humor manifest. Having secured the truck in the lot, we push off into the water just as dawn lightens the sky.

The wide channel was carved out of the Everglades by the Army Corps of Engineers years ago; it's straight path incongruous with the wild surroundings. Sitting up front, I scan the smooth water ahead of us. Occasionally I spy matted-down grass along the banks where alligators have lain, and a few wading birds take flight as we head south. No other boats are present. We are alone with nature. I pull my jacket tight against my lean frame, grateful for the buff that hugs my neck. Aside from the morning chill, there is no threat of inclement weather to hinder us today.

After some time, the waterway makes a great sweeping turn to the left and the sound of our motor quiets. Our pace slows. I turn around with a questioning look, noticing the wake we've drawn begin to bunch up and widen. Garrett's not looking in the direction of the channel, but toward his right. Following his gaze, I only see dense vegetation bordering the water. And then, a small opening, no larger than the width of the boat. Slowly, we turn in that direction.

My heart starts beating fast as we near the mangroves and my eyebrows press up together. I glance back at Garrett but determination shows in his face, his green eyes steady.

"Where are you going?" I ask, my fingers clutching the gunwale. "This doesn't look like a river."

Looking directly at me, he matter-of-factly says, "Don't worry."

I don't really have a choice but to let him lead, taking me into this wild area that he knows better than I do.

I swivel around to the left one last time and watch with trepidation as the channel from which we'd just come disappears, the dark tropical forest swallowing us. This "river" is not used by anyone as far as I can tell. It's a secret place. The brown watery path is wreathed in green waxy leaves and occasionally ripples with the swoosh of a fish's tail. How does Garrett expect us to get through here? Twisted limbs scrape the sides of the boat and hang over our heads in a low canopy. I duck down. Our progress slows. At some points, knobby roots are bent so high and tight that we need to get out, stand on top of them, and pull the wobbling boat and motor forward to wider water.

My anxiety grows as we push inward, deep into the thicket. Suddenly I am overwhelmed by one single thought: Where are the spiders? I scan every branch and clearing for webs, my body crouching down to avoid any possible contact with them. I keep the neck of my jacket zipped high. You would think that having spent my childhood playing in an old barn that I would have no care about crawling creatures. I grew up jumping on musty haybales, ducking behind cobwebbed rabbit cages, climbing to a dusty loft, and hiding in discarded vehicles. Spiders, bugs, and bats lived in the crevices that my fingers sought for support. The laughter from childhood must have overridden any concerns I might have had back then. There is no laughter now.

The thought of an elastic web across my face, or worse, something crawling on me makes me shiver. My shoulders bunch up and my arms fold in front of me. My eyes are watchful. I wave my paddle back and forth to break apart the invisible lines that I know are there.

At times, I am forced to grab onto overhead limbs for leverage to move forward. In the densest areas I bend my body down into the front V of the little boat like a contortionist, while the mangroves drag over me, leaving little room for escape.

Through gritted teeth I say, "Garrett! What are you doing to me? Why are we doing this?"

Another low branch requires me to take cover. "Oh my God. I can't believe you're making me do this." I position my arms overhead for protection.

At this point I imagine myself lost in the middle of nowhere.

"Garrett, do we have a cell signal? Do you know where we are?"

"Mom. Relax," he says in a calming voice. "We're almost there."

"But Garrett! This is ridiculous. How do you even know this is a river? What if we get lost?" My instincts for safety are on high alert and I am getting angry. I don't trust his judgement.

A few moments later we enter a pool of water not much wider than the Gheenoe. "Garrett. Let's turn around here. We don't know where we are. There could be alligators. This might not even be a river. We don't have cell service. Please. Let's go back," I say. My voice quivers, my plea strong. When I crane my neck around, I'm reminded that we would need to repeat the same agony we had just come through to return to the channel. My spirits drop as low as the tide.

I have always tried to be a good mom, showing my love by baking homemade cookies, teaching Garrett to read, getting him the right kind of shoes. I sent him to Peru for adventure, captured his parakeets when they escaped, and even allowed him to raise tadpoles through the winter in his bedroom. So why does he not listen to me or love me equally in return? Why doesn't he honor and respect my requests? Sitting in the middle of the Everglades, my worries of getting out alive escalating, I've become an insecure and aggravating mother.

But Garrett keeps calm. He gives me a reassuring half-smile as he placates my worry with the soothing words, "Mom, we'll be there soon." I have always been the one in charge. Yet here, the roles are reversed, and he is now the confident leader. I must depend on him. When did this all happen? When did he become so mature and knowing?

This is the child I helped groom, giving him land and water as his playground. His early internet wasn't a computer; it was a bookshelf which housed nature books, animal skulls and homemade slingshots. When he was young, our TV sat idle while he designed a golf course through our wetlands, built giant tree forts beneath the pines, and caught snakes sunning themselves on rock piles. As he got older, he spent more time in a trash-picked paddle boat than he did at home.

We have a house in Marco Island which he calls home now. There, he has undergone the transformation from college student, to graduate, to full time employee, to fishing guide. His former forty-acre backyard in Michigan has been replaced by a land comprising 10,000 islands which he is getting to know almost as well. A boat, a slew of fly rods, a mash of handmade flies, and a motor are all he needs.

It dawns on me that I like this person that Garrett has become--a serious, adventurous, supposedly funny, fisherman. Realizing this, I make the choice to trust him. I resign to keep going forward with the knowledge that our destination will soon be upon us with him as our capable guide.

We motor through the tiny pond and continue back between the knobby roots and greenery. And although I still cringe at having to push and pull our way through, there is new hope. I start to appreciate this adventure. I enjoy the quietness around us. Before long, the sky that had been playing hide and seek among the leaves opens into a giant bowl of blue, and with the feeling of giving birth, we emerge into a wide world of water. It is breathtaking.

My entire body relaxes. We are in the middle of God's creation, floating across coffee colored water, surrounded by the green of the mangroves, warmed by the sun I savor the gentle current of air as I lay back in my seat gazing into the blue heavens at the wispy clouds with long white tails. A pink spoonbill flies over. The smell is familiar, non-descript, clear. This is a dream. It feels like school just let out and the whole summer vacation is before me and I don't want it to end. On any other day the weather wouldn't be this calm and the sky not as blue. I smile.

When David Attenborough said that the natural world is "the greatest source of visual beauty" he was surely talking about this hidden world, far from any person or machine. This isn't a park where hundreds of cars line the road with garrulous tourists, hoping to see nature but only finding beauty in their selfies. It's God's gift to a fisherman.

How can I hold onto this moment? I don't want to forget this feeling of awe and peacefulness. I try to soak it all in, absorbing the sunshine and planting it deep into the warm skin of my memory. Not just of being in this place but being in this place with my son.

"It's beautiful," I exclaim.

He nods in agreement. I know he feels it, too.

Garrett readies his fishing gear. His six-foot powerful body towers over me as he balances atop the platform. I listen to the whip of his line as he gracefully arcs his fly rod back and forth over my head. It's like music. He lands the perfect cast along the mangroves where he knows the snook are waiting with the sawfish. Within seconds, he pulls back the rod and it bends with the weight of a fish. Garrett's face lights up. Steadily reeling in the line, he strikes up a conversation; not with me but with the fish.

"That's enough of that buddy. No, no, no, no. Don't be like that. Come on."

It doesn't even matter the words aren't for me. The fun of watching my son in the middle of the Everglades doing what he loves most is enough. Now I understand why Garrett asked me to fish with him. He knows that no one could appreciate this as much as I do. All the frustration I have held because Garrett doesn't share himself with me evaporates. An understanding washes over me that this attachment to nature, having been forged on his being since birth, is one that I helped to create. It binds us together.

We linger for as long as we can as Garrett continues to master each cast of his fly rod, but we cannot stay forever. We eventually head out through another channel, making our way back to where the noise and hustle of civilization resides. My fear of the spidery branches disappears, like the secret lake we leave behind, and I already long to come back. I won't mention my reflections of this day to Garrett; he'll be happy for that. And I'll be happy that despite the reservations Garrett may have toward me he'll likely ask me to go fishing again. When he does, I'll mask my enthusiasm.

Toadeater with Baton

Dima Altyn

MOSCOW CENTER
UNIDENTIFIED LOCATION, RUSSIA

National security service commanders just left the war room. Inside, two intelligence agents, wearing Rolexes and smart navy-blue suits, watched the door smoothly close. They kept the silence, loaded with controversial assignments.

The decreasing rate of trust by the Russian people in the ruling power was one of the problems. The confidential report on how to boost the people's patriotism was not adopted by senior ranks and needed additional work. The agents pointlessly turned the pages of the report.

The paneled room was a secret command center, which in other countries would be more likened to a dugout. But this place was both an atomic bomb shelter, and an exhibit of the Tsar's chamber décor of the eighteenth century: a polished oak table, leather chairs the color of cognac and dried tobacco, and crystal chandeliers. It also had an escape tunnel to a suburban airport.

Both men belonged to the top-secret unit of the Russian Federal Security Service, FSB, and had personal connections within the state power elite. They didn't mind people gave them a disrespectful nickname, Faces.

Ivan Bulldoff was taller and higher in rank. Detailing top-secret operations was his specialty; most of them were intricately cunning.

Lev Shekan looked like a bespectacled nerd in his forties. He was the chief of artistic bullshitting in the Bureau, and in charge of the report that now turned into his biggest headache. His favorite saying was, "Fear and batons are the best tools to forge patriotism."

"I do not know what can be improved." Shekan was upset, "I should probably emphasize the potential impact of moral degradation from the West. Like, the US has canceled male and female differences. Russian people do not want it to happen to them!"

"I like the idea," Bulldoff grinned. "The fucking blogger, Navalny, is another problem. He became too popular writing about the Kremlin's corruption."

Shekan nodded as Bulldoff continued. "My guys in western Siberia screwed up his poisoning. The executer failed to calculate the right portion of Novichok components to have the target terminated during his S7 flight from Tomsk to Moscow. In the airport, our doctors waited with the diagnosis of severe metabolic disorder. Novichok is a beauty; leaves no trace."

"If executed correctly." Shekan sighed.

"The pilot created a problem too," Bulldoff went on. "After seeing a passenger foaming at the mouth, he landed in Omsk ignoring the tower's not-to-land order. The Omsk doctors provided Navalny with first aid, which gave the troublemaker extra time. Then in Berlin's Charité Clinic, the German intelligence guarded him as if he was a head of the state. Somehow, they managed to determine the formula of Novichok and found the right treatment. I must have their antidotes. Otherwise, my head will fly."

Bulldoff slightly raised his arms, and Shekan shivered.

"Now, when Navalny is behind bars, we have to clean up the mess," said Bulldoff, squinting and pounding his fists on the oak table. "The power elite want us to prove to the world that Novichok is not our creation; that anyone can make it, eat it and survive."

"Smart!" Shekan could not hide his cynical smile.

The image of his seventeen-year-old girlfriend appeared in Bulldoff's mind. "Champaign-gold hair down to her buttocks," he murmured before he forced himself back to the present. "Where was I? Yes, I am about to win my Tetris head-game with the German counterintelligence. Our Swastika-tattooed contacts are finally ready to sell me the findings of the German doctors."

Shekan leaned toward Bulldoff with his mouth turning up at the corners. "And I'll assist in providing expandable material, call them sacrificial lambs, who will eat Novichok in front of the camera."

"Who do you think will eat a poison?" Bulldoff's eyebrows raised.

"Ha," Shekan grinned, "they won't have a choice. The video testimony will shut up Western liberals once and for all."

"Smart!" Bulldoff was on his way to the door.

"How much is your Bentley Bacalar?" Shekan asked out of the blue.

Bulldoff gave his comrade a scornful look, "You will have to eat a lot of toads to please the power pinnacle before you can afford one like this. For now, rewrite the fucking report."

MANEZHNAYA PLAZA,
WALKING DISTANCE TO THE KREMLIN,
MOSCOW, RUSSIA

In the last week of January 2021, Russia was boiling with riots. Tens of thousands of Russians, mainly young patriots, left their flats and stepped outside to freezing streets. Some were protesting against hardening autocracy, others demanded to free Navalny. Young and handsome Pavel Crowbar had no particular goal. Not a politician, but with a strong sense of justice, he marched close to the protesters. He wanted to contribute to justice with his talent in computation and hacking according to his moral standards of social equality. Occasionally Pavel thought of himself as of a modern-day Robin Hood who, instead of arrows, shot signals via the WEB. This comparison made him feel good, as he shouted toward the Kremlin, "You are nothing but a horrible venomous cocktail of democracy and autocracy. You pretend to rule a great country but offer nothing except corruption and nepotism."

Two wardrobe-size guards, called omonovets in Russian, stepped forward and knocked Pavel down, and threw their heavy bodies on top of him. They yelled and swore, spurting tons of saliva. Two frozen rubber batons flashed in the air, up and down. Pavel gritted his teeth in pain and panted. Around them, a blazed crowd was held back by other guards who quickly built a perimeter defense line to secure Pavel's apprehension.

"Want freedom?" omonovets said to Pavel's ear. "Russia does not need freedom, it needs stability. Oligarchs' have the right to steal. They are the power!"

"Toadeaters!" Pavel kept jerking, trying to struggle away. Suddenly, he saw a face of a rogue girl next to him on the ground.

Her face was muddy, but her large eyes, plump lips, and cheeks radiated energy.

Pavel growled, "What? The morons not even spare women?"

The girl's large eyes opened even wider. "Nice meeting you."

"I am Pavel."

"Liz."

"Are you out of your mind? First, you joined the riot and then fought the Russian Guards?" The omonovets pressed harder on his back, blocking Pavel's airflow.

"Yeah," Liz said, "just like that. I hate violence."

Pavel and Liz were dragged up by many guards' arms and were pushed one after another into the paddy wagon. Pavel had a broken nose and a broken rib. His jeans were torn; blood dripped through. He saw the pretty brunette, Liz, next to him. The girl looked fine and even gave a smile to the badly beaten boy. He saw a sign of approval in her enchanting eyes. The bus moved off, tearing through the frosty Moscow evening. New acquaintances who met while kissing Mother Earth instinctively snuggled to each other.

MATROSSKAYA TISHINA PRISON
MOSCOW, RUSSIA

The long military-green corridor served as a waiting room for about one hundred detainees, who have been waiting for who knows how long to get orders from prison officers. It was torture by uncertainty.

Pavel and Liz were lucky to sit together because the three benches were given only to women and badly injured men. Liz was half-asleep on Pavel's chest when he whispered in her ear.

"The US constitution based on democratic elections came to life a hundred years before the abolition of serfdom in Russia. Think about it. It took the Russians one hundred years to decide on whether to say good riddance to feudalism."

"How do you know all shit?" Liz moaned; her eyes closed.

"I am smart."

"I like smart men."

"I'm gonna beat them with my clever programs, just like they beat me with batons."

"Fire!" Liz shrieked as the corners of her lips turned up.

It was only three inches for Liz's lips to reach Pavel's. She shifted and gave him a heavenly kiss: soft, wet and vibrating. She embraced him with a magic female's heat, even if it happened in the devilish place where feelings were as appropriate as in the coffin.

As if to confirm evil was near, the sound of police batons drumming on plastic shields disturbed the air. The jailors began calling names and sorting detainees.

"Liz, I need a partner; I have a job to do. It's dangerous," Pavel whispered to the plucky spirited girl whose charm and bravery embraced his heart.

"You are a curious piece of work… count me in. You remember my number, yes?" Liz clung to Pavel so close that he felt her heartbeat.

With the baton out in front of him, a jailor appeared between them. "Liz Stone, leave now!"

Soon only Pavel was sitting in the monstrous corridor. There was no food, not even water. To kill time, Pavel thought about his plan to hack into the jail's network and free all political prisoners. He knew, though, if he plays this risky game with oligarchs and security forces, he better hit big.

"You, the handsome one! Pavel Crowbar!" The man who called Pavel handsome wasn't a detention officer. It was easy for Pavel to determine that the man was a Face. Even if they could read my mind, it would be too fast for them to send an agent to stop my hacking. A light smile crossed Pavel's lips.

"You smile. You like it here?"

"Not at all. It was a dream."

"What about?"

"Women!"

"We noticed you lovey-dovey with Liz Stone. She is not your type. Margaret Thatcher is your type." The Face chuckled.

"Thanks," Pavel said dryly.

The Face took Pavel to the second floor below ground designated for enemies of the state. The elevator was the industrial size, loud and slow. Nobody knew when it was added to the two-story barrack-type hospital erected in 1775. Looking like a large prison cell, the elevator must have witnessed countless wrongful deaths.

The Face knocked on a metal door and let the detainee

in. Ivan Bulldoff and Lev Shekan met Pavel in a warehouse-size room. From a distance, they showed their secret service IDs.

"Call me Ivan," said the bigger one. "And he is Lev."

The two Faces first threatened Pavel with years in prison for injuring two or three omonovets; then offered a deal. Cold-hearted, they offered Pavel to ingest a non-harmful — as they called it — dose of Novichok in a German lab. The Faces would control and videotape the process in case of complications. They promised to administer the antidote. Seeing Pavel firmly shake his head, the Faces, offered to pay him $425K after swallowing the substance, and the same amount again after the interview.

Pavel felt as if he had been hit by lightning. "Are you fuck-ing serious?" Tiny pearls of sweat appeared on Pavel's forehead. He stood speechless.

Lev offered stoned Pavel a chair, a glass of water, a turkey sandwich, leaving behind a plume of exotic cologne.

5 FILYUVSKY STREET,
FIRST FLOOR
WORKING-CLASS SUBURBAN MOSCOW

Pavel made the deal with the Faces. He had to buy time. It was clear they had an operation to carry out, and they choose Pavel as the expendable 'volunteer'. Keeping him alive was not in their plan.

Shortly he was in the doorway of Anna's apartment — his elderly neighbor and good friend. Anna's face was enlightened with a smile. Pavel stepped in and, without wasting time, ar-ranged on the fridge shelves the yummy treats he bought for Anna: grass-fed chicken, honey-sour-creamed cottage cheese, carrot cake, and an imported Brazilian watermelon. The woman began to bustle in the kitchen, while Pavel picked up the land-line phone and dialed Liz's number.

"You!" Liz gasped for breath. "Where are you?"

"Look, I do not have time. I traded my life for freedom. Now I have to fight for it."

"What did you do?"

"I'll tell you later. I need your help"

"I already said 'yes'."

"I must have a ten-milligram glass vial of Novichok,

variant A-234. It's an organophosphate nerve agent. Also, two antidotes; one is galantamine, another — atropine."

"Where did you learn this shit?"

"I took a crash course from a smuggler. He owed me for teaching his people the basics of hacking the Core Banking Solution network."

"You are more dangerous than I thought."

"Liz!"

"What do you want me to do?"

"You need to pay a visit to the source, Doctor Death. He is a chemist, Leo Rink, at the Science Institute for Organic Chemistry in Shikhany. In the 90s he and his assistant Zoya Koshel sold Novichok as easily as if it was candy. Shikhany, the military-industrial settlement, is in the middle of nowhere. A special pass is needed to get through the checkpoint. Fly to Saratov. Check-in a lux room at The Pearl hotel on Cathedral Square. Hire a jeep with an experienced driver; you will have to survive the two-hundred-mile round trip between Saratov and Shikhany over icy, bumpy roads."

"How will I find the chemical weapon sellers? Look in ads?"

"Start with Zoya; she sings with a chorus of veterans. The name of the chorus is like Hello, My Song! As for the rest — be creative."

"Holy shit! They gonna give me what you want just because I am a pretty woman?"

"No, I'll send you enough money."

"That's it?"

"No. I am under surveillance. No more contact with me. Change the SIM card, text me, and I'll text you back with instructions. If everything works the way I plan, I'll see you in a couple of days in Berlin."

Liz's deep sigh came over the telephone line.

"Something more." Pavel whispered, "You are the only one. Take care of yourself. I'll not live without you. It is deadly serious."

"See you!"

From the kitchen, Anna brought a tray with snacks and green tea.

Pavel hugged her. "My dear, I do not have time for tea. I need to borrow some money from you."

"How much?"

"All you have."

"OK" Anna was already on her way to the wardrobe where Russian women keep the banknotes in cylindrical rolls.

"Anna, look… I've got a job and need to travel overseas. I sold my flat upstairs. Do you remember my classmate, Michael, the realtor? He'll bring the money to you tomorrow. It's yours."

"I do not need this money." Anna bowed her head tears filling her eyes. "I understand. Will you ever come back to visit me?"

"Yes, I promise."

The old lady, pure of heart and a survivor, stood in front of Pavel. Her shaking hands pressed the crumpled banknotes into his hands. It was all her life savings. For Pavel Crowbar, there could be no higher authority in the world than the behest of this woman.

"When you come next time, I'll finish the story about how your mom and how I escaped, purely by chance, the German Nazi's bomb that destroyed the flat you sold."

"Yes, I will always love you as my second mom."

Anna's tears kept dropping. Still, her face glowed with pride for Pavel. She bowed deeply and blessed Pavel by making a cross with her hand in the air.

"Let God keep you safe."

INSTITUTE FOR ORGANIC CHEMISTRY
AND TECHNOLOGY
SHIKNANY SARATOV REGION, RUSSIA

At midnight, Liz's airplane touched down at the Saratov airport. A taxi whisked her to the hotel minutes later. Saratov was nowhere close to Moscow in size and ambience. Since the mid-nineteenth century, Russian literature referred to this place as something remote and dull. Still, the Pearl hotel was decent, even if a little pretentious.

Liz took the penthouse room, which was spacious and had a private sauna. She peeled off her plain shirt and jeans before washing her face; all the while thinking, It was a wise decision to refrain from sexy make-up and eye-catching clothes.

In the morning, she hired a car. The Jeep Cherokee came with a driver who looked like a disappointed landlord upset by low rent. However, when he agreed to find the witchy-singer Zoya Koshel at no extra, Liz changed her opinion of the guy. Dip-shit the driver knew of Zoya. She was obviously a local star.

The driver spun the car as if he was competing in Formula One. But soon he abruptly stopped in the center of the town. Surprised, Liz looked around. There was a bakery, passport photoshop, and a quaint little bookshop along the street. Why?

"Buy the book," the driver said.

"I do not need any book."

"Buy The Collection of Popular Russian Folk Song."

"I am not singing!"

"Do you want Zoya's attention? Book is a present for her."

"I got it, thanks." Liz jumped out of the car and quickly returned with a book.

The driver started the car to continue racing. Soon Liz saw no more buildings along the road, only a vast steppe covered with snow. Uneven pavers and ice beneath the snow made the trip torture. Halfway through their journey, the car plunged into the snow and bogged.

"Get out!" the driver's low wheezing voice sounded.

"What?"

"I said get out, push on the rear bumper."

"Wow." Liz jumped into knee-deep snow and pushed with her full strength. The car was throwing out the massive exhaust. The wheels skidded in the snow with a jarring squeal. Exhausted and cold from her hair to her toes, Liz could not stand the gusting wind any longer. She climbed into the warm car and curled up on the back seat, instantly falling asleep. Soon, the powerful sound of a tractor woke her. Shortly, the Jeep was out of the massive snowdrift, and Liz felt a jerk as the wheels sharply gripped the pavers. The driver pushed the gas pedal to its limit.

Jersey barriers painted white with red stripes blocked the entrance to the restricted settlement. From a small plywood shed, four military guards in green-brown-black camouflage uniforms rolled out. They were of short in stature, wore oversized jackets, and carried Kalashnikov assault rifles. One guard had two Kalashnikovs that hung on his narrow shoulders like on a wardrobe hanger.

The driver said something as he was getting out of the car. Surrounded by guards he quickly disappeared inside the shed.

Liz's temperature raised, and her heart pounded so hard like it was about to jump out of her chest. Her palms and armpits sweated profusely. She did not know what to say to the guards, had no idea what the driver told, and could not foresee how the guards would act. The one thing she knew was that Pavel would be in grave danger if she did not bring the antidote.

The driver opened the door, letting frost into the interior. "Five hundred greens."

"Will they take rubles?" Liz threw out instinctively a bridge not knowing if it was a good move.

"Greens."

Liz paid the asking price. As the car started moving, she exhaled with relief. It was a bad idea to negotiate with Kalashnikov bearers. The birthplace of Novichok appeared on the left. It was a four-story building of prefabricated concrete blocks. The driver quickly passed the building as if he feared nerve poison might come spilling out. After a couple of turns along crooked streets, the Jeep entered a residential barrack area; then stopped at the far end of a dull Khrushchev-era building and hid behind industrial size rusted garbage containers. Liz turned her eyes away from the ugly, stinky plastic bags, which spilled over and clung to the sides. The driver left the car and returned swiftly with an elderly woman — real Russian babushka who energetically opened the back door and dropped her body on the seat. She wore a woolen scarf over her head that slid down to her right ear. Uncombed, oily strands of hair stuck out from her scarf.

Liz moved father to the door on her side. "Are you Zoya?"

"Yes, I have been Zoya all the years I lived." The babushka grabbed the book from Liz's hands, then, looking at the title page, opened her mouth wide with only a couple of teeth as if she was about to sing an aria. Instead, she addressed her customer in a business-like manner.

"Two thousand greens. It's my cut. Doctor Death, Rink has retired. Instead, you'll see his nephew, Fyodor. His cut may be a bit higher."

"OK. But I need Novichok A-234 and two antidotes with a liquid carrier in ten-milligram clear glass vials. Understood?'

The babushka nodded. Liz handed Zoya her cut.

"How will I meet Fyodor?"

"Tonight. Wait in your room."

"What time?"

"Tonight. He looks strange."

"What do you mean?"

"The beard… locals call him Terrorist."

Back in The Pearl, it was close to midnight when Liz opened the door to a bald man with a bin Laden beard. He wore a thobe-like coat, oversized shirt, and pants, all in black.

It was Terrorist. He approached Liz as if she was a streetwalker. A waiter with the best champagne and exotic fruits followed him to the room. The guest drank a whole glass of champagne, not even glancing in Liz's direction. Then he set three vials on the table.

"I got what you asked for — A-234 and the two complimenting antidotes: popular choice. Ha-ha. All three are in clear vials, as you asked."

"The price Zoya mentioned is steep. I could have gotten the same in Slovakia for half the money." Liz did not have a clue what she was saying.

"It's not expensive, and you have not heard it all yet."

"What do you mean?"

"Ten milligrams of A-234 alone costs the US $6,000. And you'll get it free if you give me a good head job and a fuck. For short ten minutes, you'll get as much money as streetwalkers earn in a month of hard work."

"Hmm… And if I say, 'fuck yourself?'"

"It'll be very rude." Terrorist made a step to where he hung his coat and pulled out of the scabbard affixed to the lining, a short Arabic saber. The saber's sharp curved edge reflected the light of the chandelier directly in Liz's eyes.

"Hmm…" Liz tried to stay calm steering the guy in the direction she needed. "OK! You look like a nice guy."

"Yeah. But don't make me wait." Terrorist raised his voice, losing cool.

"I'll do it. Only for you." A theatrical whisper came from Liz's corner.

There were about ten feet between the table where Terrorist stood and the chair where Liz sat. Liz's mind was on fire. She assessed the distance for her counterattack, which was imminent. There were only seconds to plan. Liz touched a ten-milligram vial filled with vinegar, which she kept in her pocket. Terrorist came closer to Liz, stretching his long Gorilla-arms to her. The girl raised her right leg and pressed it against his genitals, holding him back. He lost momentum. His eyes widened; his lips curved in surprise as a sharp convulsion possessed his body.

"Oh, babe…"

Terrorist liked what Liz did because it looked like a painless, sexy game. In anticipation, his mouth chewed the air and discharged a stream of saliva.

"Stay! Do not move!" Slowly, teasingly Liz released the belt on her jeans. She stretched to her full height and opened her shoulders while protruding her pubis forward. An inch of Liz's eclectic-red panties was enough to send the man's head spinning.

"Turn around and go sit on the upper bunk of the sauna. Keep the door open. I'll slowly walk over to give you a pleasure you never experienced before." She whispered in a poisonous sweet voice.

Terrorist turned into a feeble piece of flesh. With his trousers and underwear lowered to his knees, the man moved in short steps to the sauna. Looking at his buttocks wobbling like jelly, Liz felt just as disgusted with the man's ass as with his face.

"I'll play you with my lips and tongue," said Liz putting her hands on the man's inner thighs. Just then, seeing his crooked stick with a red pimple at its end, Liz sprang to immediate attack.

With a quick move, she pulled a vial out of her pocket, which looked exactly like Terrorist's vial with Novichok, and poured the substance on the man's junk.

Terrorist yelled insanely. "Ah! What did you do! You — bitch, the whole hotel will die. You too…" He tried to jump away, but it was too late. Liz smashed the sauna's cedar bucket on his head.

The man's eyes rolled back behind his eyelids as his body dropped down to the floor. Pantless, but with his shirt still on, he curled his body and rooted moaning in pain. Liz poured the rest of the vinegar from the vial on his bleeding skull and returned the vial to her pocket, Nobody gonna die in the hotel tonight. Even you, dumb prick.

In lightning speed, Liz grabbed three vials from the table. She still could catch the early morning flight from Saratov to Moscow.

Pavel sat at the hotel bar and drank soda to an obvious dissatisfaction of the bartender. He was practicing his comprehension of German by listening to a group of cheerful men with Nazi swastika tattoos. They talked about something related to the art of tattoos. Pavel knew Nazi symbols were illegal in Germany unless they contained artistry. The law is kind of tricky.

On his way out, Pavel heard the Germans laugh so loudly that their noise echoed in the elevator with the doors closed.

Upstairs, when Liz entered the room, Pavel opened his arms long before she stepped close. Hugging on each other, they spent minutes in silence. Their hearts jumped with joy, but the tongues refused to move. Pavel wanted to see and feel the woman who had gone through hell and returned in one piece. He kept gently stroking her hair, touched her cheeks, neck, and shoulders. At that moment, between them there was no reward, nor gratitude; only love and care, only heavenly kisses. With rocket speed, Liz's cobalt blue panties flew to the corner. Naked bodies intertwined for only a short festivity of love.

"We'll have our quality time. Later. I promise," said Pavel ordering protein dinner to the room.

They ate, drank a red 1982 Boudreaux, and planned for the next day. Pavel's computer-like brain elaborated on a second-by-second plan.

"The Faces use me as a piece of meat to show the world that fools like Navalny and I eat Novichok to discredit Kremlin. On the other hand, they want to demonstrate to German extremists the effectiveness of Novichok. In exchange, the Faces want the antidote formula Germans employed to cure Navalny. They will try to dispose of me as soon as the video is made."

"But we are smarter than they are, aren't we?"

"Yeah, first, I took the antidotes you brought. By the way, galantamine helps in treating Alzheimer's."

"I'll keep it in mind," said Liz.

"Tomorrow we will pray the antidotes to work on the type of Novichok the bastards are giving me. The event will take place in a secret room adjacent to a huge morgue 07XU. Its walls have lots of refrigerated drawers holding corpses. I reprogrammed all hospital departments to use 07XU as the only destination as of tomorrow. The time of my Novichok-eating session is set for 4:00 p.m. You detonate a smoke-bomb precisely at 4:30 p.m."

"Will dead people help us?" Liz asked.

Pavel offered no answer.

Soon, after midnight Pavel and Liz's eyes closed and they fell asleep holding each other's hands.

MORGUE 07XU
BERLIN, GERMANY

Pavel and the Face met on the designated spot in a tunnel-like corridor leading to 07XU. The Face wore white garb and respiratory mask covering most of his face. He put a garb on Pavel and took him to the secret lab. When they crossed the huge morgue, Pavel estimated there were two hundred cells with dead bodies calmly resting under refrigeration. The Face dropped onto his arms and knees, opened a low-clearance door that was camouflaged as a morgue cell, and crawled into the adjacent room; Pavel followed him. Inside there was another man dressed in a white garb with an eye-catching swastika tattoo on a side of his neck. The tattooed man held two vials in his hands. If anything goes against my plan I will be dead in minutes, Pavel thought. The tension in the air and the presence of dead bodies in the morgue could drive even a warrior insane. And yet, Pavel stayed cool. He breathed deeply, focusing on what he needed to do, rather than on his death.

"You, Novichok Eater, move your ass over here!" The tattooed man yelled with a German accent.

"I take the poison and you transfer the advance right away," said Pavel, opening his laptop.

"You do not trust us." The Face said stepping closer to Pavel.

"The deal was US $425K immediately after I swallow the poison and another US $425K as soon as the ten-minute video is complete."

"Ha!" Playful notes were in the Face's voice. "You will not survive that long."

"It should not be your concern," said Pavel looking straight into the Face's eyes.

"Playing tough... What if you eat the poison but

we do not pay?"

Pavel was ready for this turn. "You'll get another corpse in this morgue, and your bosses, Ivan and Lev will tear your balls apart."

"Fuck you. Doctor, please see the patient," said the Face; the whites of his eyes turned blood-red.

The liquid flew over Pavel's tongue and slid down to the stomach and the intestines, aiming at doing deadly damage. When attacking receptors, which mediate functions of the nervous system, Novichok bumped into a rubber wall of antidotes that stopped the poison's penetration to the brain like condoms block unwanted sperm. Pavel sighed. Should I feel optimistic? His laptop screen showed the transaction was successful. Pavel, quickly seeing that no one was watching, touched several keys, paused, and then pressed enter. His proprietary worm was sent to the sender's account in the transacting bank. Novichok Eater became the new owner of the FSB's account.

The time was 4:29. It was a "go." Just then, the electricity went off. A hospital siren indicating urgent evacuation sounded, followed by a muffled explosion behind the door. The man with the swastika crawled outside. There he screamed in horror. Clouds of smoke billowed into the lab. The FSB agent put his gun to Pavel's head and pushed him down on all fours. He was going crazy realizing that he was trapped and could do nothing except force Pavel through the opening. He kept pushing the Novichok Eater's buttocks with his gun's muzzle.

"The exit is blocked by stretchers." Pavel crawled backward, punching the man with his buttocks.

"Get the fuck out!"

In the next instance, Pavel twisted his body, slipped underneath the stretcher, and disappeared into the foggy morgue room.

"You, son of a bitch, where are you? Do not play games with me." When the Face finally got outside, he smacked his chest hard against the metal edge of the stretcher and bent deep, almost kissing the skull of a dead body. The smash leveraged the skeleton to motion, first to sit up, and then to drop back down on the stretcher, sending the white sheet flying over on the Face's head. The dead body was just skin and bones. Its ice-cold left arm swung in the air and landed on the FSB agent's arm, holding the gun.

"It's mine!" the agent screamed, tearing the sheet off his head. The noise made by the corpse helped Liz to guide her weapon, the Raid Roach Killer, and to spray it directly into the agent's eyes, who yelled even louder. It was a sign that the officer was no longer fit for devilish duties. Liz's club knocked him down. The agent managed to fire a shot that hit the corpse making it jump again. On the floor, the agent cried like a child who was about to lose a bet.

Liz and Pavel had already crawled under the stretchers using smoke and the ocean of stretchers to their advantage. Liz helped Pavel who was short of breath.

"Did you program this shit?" asked Liz. "All dead people in one room?"

"You don't like my plan?"

"It's scary. I do not want them to haunt me in my dreams."

"Don't worry. The place in your dreams is already taken."

Hundreds of policemen were surrounding the building, and it would be only minutes before they discovered the alarm was false. All exits would be shut down. So, Liz and Pavel ran hard and soon they found the entrance to the ventilation ducting system and squeezed in through a narrow window. Coming out the other side, the two finally saw daylight. Tired and scratched all over, they stood leaning one against the other.

Pavel's face was pale. He needed an additional dose of antidotes.

TOP-FLOOR CONDOMINIUM UNIT
SKYLINE ROSE GARDENS
LONDON, ENGLAND

In the spacious living room, Liz and Pavel sat on a silky sofa. The luxurious apartment they bought offered 180 degrees of panoramic view of the city. To the east, they could see the Lloyds Bank's futuristic architecture. Historic districts were to the west. The iconic seventeen century St. Paul's Cathedral and Buckingham Palace gave joy to their eyes and food to their brain.

For a while, Pavel enjoyed looking at Lloyds's inside-out building where all communications and lifts have been attached to the outside of the structure.

"Extraordinary architecture. What we did, Liz is also surreal," he said closing his super-powerful laptop. "It wasn't a big deal to hack the Russian Bank that Faces used to finance the Novichok Eater operation. Now the secret service monsters that eat toads to please the oligarchs' ruling will see the deficit of ninety million dollars. Let Lloyds's capitalists keep this bloody money for a while. Quietly we'll return the money to Russian hospitals and kindergartens."

"Toadeaters, this is our The Robin Hoodian Act of Justice!" Liz smiled, "I see now what you meant yelling toadeaters when we first met lying in the mud on Manezhnaya Plaza."

She leaned back against the cushions, examining the firmness of the pricey Italian handmade Natuzzi furniture. Her thin fingers twirled her glass of crisp Chardonnay.

"Yeah, money? Hollywood annoys me with the cliché showing smiling faces with bags of cash," she directed her words to the window. "I don't feel any happier because of the money. You make me happy. One question though."

"What else do you want to know, my dear?"

"I understand about antidotes but why did you need Novichok A-234?"

"Hmm. You never know," Pavel looked at Liz. Now, his thoughts were not about death, they were about love. "You are the smartest, the bravest, and the most beautiful girl Hollywood could ever imagine."

Liz caught Pavel's gentleness. Pavel stepped closer to Liz, who stood. He slowly and gently put his arms around her shoulders. They kissed leisurely, yet deeply and passionately. Pavel detached himself from his lover and looked at her beauty from arm's length. Their eyes celebrated the moment of their unity. Then Pavel pulled her closer so that he sensed her breath and full breasts flattening against his chest. His growing manhood shoved against her pubis. In harmonic response, her body shivered from electricity. They smiled, enjoying the moment, sensing sweet ecstasy to come.

What If It's You?

D.F. Dawson

Dr. Seuss of children's book fame said we often do not fully appreciate the impact of a moment until we view it as a memory. One such moment occurred for me because I agreed to shepherd my wife's karate group on an early Fall bike ride. Since many of them had not ridden much, she asked if I would accompany them as an experienced cyclist. The plan for after the ride was a pool party at a karate student's home, and then that evening, everyone would return to the same home for a potluck dinner.

My Dr. Seuss moment that day was meeting Sandra. She and her family were hosting the pool and dinner parties. I was toweling off after a dip in the pool and heard my wife say from behind, "D.F., I'd like you to meet Sandra. She and her kids are all karate students." I turned around and was caught completely off guard.

I cannot tell you if I stopped breathing, or for how long I could not respond. I know I fought to regain an assemblance of composure since my insides had just been scrambled. Whatever happened in that moment I knew was not good. My reaction was deep and dangerous because I was married and did not want such a response toward any woman save my wife. While Sandra was admittedly attractive, the feeling I had transcended the physical. It was as if my entire being, body, mind, and soul, was being pulled on by an irresistible force.

When my wife and I returned home, I tried to think of a reason for not going back for dinner. In no uncertain terms, I did not need to be around a woman who could create such a strong response in me. I had no desire to stray from my marriage. Yet, failing to come up with a reasonable excuse, we returned to Sandra's home for the potluck. Throughout the evening, I did my best to stay away from her. Yet, try as I might, anytime she appeared I could not look away.

I survived the evening and was grateful my wife did not

detect anything amiss. I breathed a sigh of relief. I was proud of myself and, at the same time, unnerved. I had been around beautiful women, could appreciate them, and let it go at that. My response to Sandra went far beyond her attractiveness to something I could not logically explain.

The months rolled by and the incident with Sandra was forgotten until Christmas. On top of my small pile of gifts was an envelope containing a gift certificate for five personal training sessions with none other than Sandra. My wife explained that Sandra discovered her husband was cheating on her, and she and the three kids had moved to a small home north of town. Sandra was looking to build her training clientele since she needed to work from home. I did my best to thank my wife for such a wonderful gift while I scrambled to figure out how not to use it. Unfortunately, my wife was thrilled she had found what she thought was the perfect gift for me. It was abundantly clear; I was going to be using the gift certificate.

Early the next year, I met with Sandra. We spent the better part of an hour discussing my physical activities and my training goals. She concluded I really did not need a personal trainer since my athletic endeavors, while focused on cycling also included running and weight training. I thought just maybe our conversation had let me off the hook. I could surrender my gift certificate, and I would have something to tell my wife about why I would not be doing personal training with Sandra – potential crisis averted. However, that is not what happened.

Instead, Sandra asked if I would be willing to use my gift certificate for massage therapy. She explained she was finishing massage school and needed people to work on to become certified. My five sessions would be sufficient for me to provide an evaluation about her as a therapist. From our conversation, she knew I had experience with massage therapy and so could serve as a knowledgeable reviewer. She added she would appreciate any feedback I would be willing to share with her.

The irony was, I had just fired my massage therapist, so I needed exactly what she was offering because I was being hampered by a nagging left leg problem. The looming question, could I handle having Sandra as my massage therapist? A brief, but intense internal battle ensued. It was like dealing with the two proverbial devils, one on each shoulder. One told me having her as my massage therapist would be one of the dumbest things I could do and I could be putting much of my life at risk. The other devil told me here was someone asking for my help with her training, offering what I needed, and I was man enough to handle the situation. It would only be for five sessions and then it would be over. That would give me time to find a different therapist. The latter devil won out and, with significant trepidation, I agreed to use my certificate for massage work.

Turned out, as a former college track athlete, Sandra was a gifted and knowledgeable therapist able to help me with my chronic cycling related problems. As a result, once my gift certificate ran out, I became her client. While I had worked with massage therapists before, never had I been attracted to any of them. To Sandra, I was merely a friend's husband and massage client. For me, it was a whole new experience. My attraction to her did not wain as I hoped. Being close to her felt like being enveloped in warmth and tenderness. Over the ensuing months, I learned a lot about self-control and keeping things on a completely professional basis. What I was feeling toward her was mine to deal with because the boundaries were clear, and I honored them.

The following year, my wife decided she wanted to get a Ph.D. and was accepted into an extremely good program at a distant university some 700 miles away. She thought it would be fine to come back home during vacations and an occasional weekend. I was far less enthusiastic about her plan. We had been in marriage counseling for a while and were not making progress with being able to communicate more effectively. Her desire to spend four or more years living away from me seemed like a decision point. After many emotionally charged discussions, we decided upon a divorce.

Post-divorce, I continued as Sandra's client, became her friend, and a few years later, we tried dating. It came about because I asked her if she would be willing to consider changing our relationship. I finally admitted to my feelings for her and how I reacted the first time we met. It was clear it was a huge risk to reveal my love and attraction. She had never signaled anything more than us being friends.

She agreed to try, but I knew it was a long shot. She had been deeply hurt by the failure of her marriage and was focused on raising her three children. In some of our previous discussions, she shared her lack of interest in being involved with anyone ever again. Logically, me asking to date her was foolish, but I had to try. If nothing else, my feelings were finally out on the table.

As well as we got along and enjoyed each other's company, Sandra was never comfortable dating me. I could sense her withdraw every time there was a hint of intimacy. Even holding my hand was an effort. Only a few weeks after our dating experiment commenced, it was finished. She admitted she just could not do it.

With a heavy heart, I did my best to embrace our relationship for what it was, an incredible friendship. I appreciated that she did not pull away after knowing my feelings, and as a result, I learned a lot about love. It was about how much I could love her, or someone like her, without any expectations, or so I believed.

About ten years after our initial pool encounter, I received my first invitation to visit Sandra's family home. Both her brother and father were facing significant health challenges. I assumed she invited me along to provide some emotional support.

Being with her and her parents felt far too comfortable and my original, overwhelming feelings came flooding back. Instead of having been diminished, as I had hoped, my attraction to her had only been buried. Knowing her desire not to be involved with me, my biggest concern was screwing up the friendship we shared by still being deeply in love with her.

Following our visit with Sandra's family, we met for dinner, and I shared what I was feeling while being with her and her family. I wanted to make sure I did not damage our relationship and took complete responsibility for my feelings. I ended by saying I hoped she would find someone with whom she could open her heart, and I could be their friend. I held my breath hoping she was not going to tell me that given my confession, it was best if we no longer spent time together. It was the outcome I desperately wanted to avoid. There was silence and then she said, "What if that person is You?" In that moment, I was not sure whether my heart stopped or was about to burst.

As it turned out, that person was me for several years. Through Sandra, I had the opportunity to experience her family, her three children, and three cats. As for the felines, I learned I could love them as much as dogs (please do not tell my former canines). We moved to an intentional community that included an organic farm, a focus on the arts, and a deep appreciation for the natural environment. Together we discovered a cooperative style of living neither of us had previously experienced, and I was not sure was even possible. The community also afforded me the opportunity to be involved with two non-profit organizations helped me develop a greater sense of serving others.

Sadly, while Sandra and I were perfectly matched on many of life's dimensions, such as finances, politics, and spirituality, having a safe emotional connection was elusive. Try as we might, we were never able to create the enduring bond to face life's challenges together.

Humans are incredibly complicated, and Sandra and I were no exceptions. Ultimately, we took different paths. Mine brought me to Southwest Florida where I hit the restart button on my life. At the southernmost elbow of Interstate 75, I set down roots in a subtropical climate with lots of water. What I found was much more than a paddler's paradise. A supportive spiritual community and a writer's group were unexpected gifts.

Although Sandra and I were not forever partners, I will always be grateful for the amazing things she brought into my life. The most important one was to open me up to a more inclusive form of love – what many call unconditional love.

Dr. Seuss was correct, I would never have guessed how much that moment of meeting Sandra would eventually change my life.

FLASH FICITON

In Your Own Voice:
How Flash Fiction and a Writing Prompt
speaks to a storyteller's voice

Ever wonder what a writing group is about? At one monthly meeting, Marco Island Writers' members were given a short, simple prompt and asked to craft a story in a genre in which they typically don't write. A fifteen-minute timer was set and the writers scribbled on.

Two of our writers, Dr. Dolores Burton and Melody Highman chose the same prompt. The prompt began with this:

"The townhouse door opened. A woman and her beloved dog stepped outside."

They later edited and polished their stories as flash fiction pieces for this anthology. Flash fiction is generally considered to be under 1000 words, a very, very short story. The variations in each story will surprise you and illustrate the distinctness of an individual storyteller's voice and how it informs a story's tone and style. Other writers in our flash fiction section chose to use a prompt, dream or idea of their own.

Melody Highman, Anthology Editorial Board

Pót San
(Blood Door, Haitian Creole)

Nancy Murvine

First, he hated himself for having painted the door red. But Gosder had to feed his growing family, and the old wood door of the rectory in their little Haitian village needed repair. "A good paint will protect it better," he had offered the priest. The color choice had been the priest's -- the Christian's blessed color of the Holy Spirit; to Haitian's, the evil color of the devil's eyes. He had been warned.

Gosder watched his pregnant wife tenderly care for the rector's garden before entering through that blood-red door sixty-six times to cook the priest's meals and clean his messes. Ashamed, he would not warn her about the curse his painted door placed on her, but silently he counted each closing like a ticking clock until, as he feared, she died. He knew in his heart that the cursed door, not the labor, led to the bleeding that took her life and led to the second thing he hated: the daughter who survived.

Growing up, Ayida never understood her father's violent outbursts which sometimes left welts that melted into black pools across her arms and legs. The nuns never investigated the reason for her long sleeves and pants worn on even the hottest days. Modesty, of course, need not be questioned. By the time Ayida turned fifteen, her little village had abandoned the Catholic church for voodoo beliefs more aligned with their African identity, and Ayida's father had abandoned her too.

Instead of feeling deserted, she felt liberated. She moved into the vacant rectory with its brilliant red door, the one her father had told her she was never to enter. Never. It was his insistence that fueled her disobedience and now declared her independence. He would not touch her here with his omens of doom or his fists of anger.

Ayida cultivated the surrounding land, resurrecting the medicinal plants that had been abandoned since her mother's death. Fey lougawou and catmint crowded the garden. The flame red flowers of quassia and castor oil plants waved like defiant flags from her little hilltop refuge where her reputation as a gangas, the village healer, likewise took root.

Here too is where she watched the decades pass and her father grow more drunken and hunched with time.

One late afternoon on a warm January day, Ayida was dividing verbena in the side garden. The soft cast of the sun's lowering light on the front door reminded her it needed painting, its pale pink a long way from its former blaring red. "Nothing threatening there," she chided herself, trying to set aside a growing sense of foreboding that had left her uneasy since morning. The day had begun with blackbirds singing before dawn; and, in their voices, she heard traces of her father's teachings to beware of this-or-that dark omen. Still, when something told her to look up, she knew it was a sign. She looked to see her father stagger to the foot of the path that wound to the rectory door. He had never come this close before. She watched as he removed his baseball cap, twisting it mercilessly in his hands. When Ayida stood, he called her mother's name. "Maffi, my girl."

Suddenly, the ground began to tremble. Ayida instinctively dropped to the dirt, desperately trying to tether herself to the earth that shook all life, like prey in savage jaws. She watched her father's frenzied lurching and his cruel fall. Below them, village houses flattened in waves of crumbling concrete blocks. All around were sounds she had never heard, roaring and anguished.

Then the earth took a breath. In the stillness, she raced to her father. He was smaller than she remembered, his sinewy frame more like a child's. She lifted him easily, wrapped his arm around her neck, and he limped painfully up the hill to her front door. "Never," he whispered when she put her hand on its iron handle.

"Never ends now," she whispered back and opened the door.

Through the nights and days of aftershocks, the injured knocked on the red door and were healed. Government rationalized structural integrity foretold life or death and began new construction. Religion claimed a miracle and reopened the church. The villagers listened only to the echoing voices of the dead for an explanation of their survival: Ayida and the red door.

Gosder would insist on repainting the door, dipping his brush into the bucket of blood-red paint, a personal sacrament of thanks to his daughter Ayida. The village would insist on changing her name, forever forward affectionately calling her Loa Pót San, Saint of the Red Door.

provided by Cindy Pierce, Florida Weekly

What's in a Name?

Nancy Murvine

Matilda liked names and she especially liked hers. Not Mattie or Tilly which was plain silly. Matilda. With stringent politeness, she would remind anyone who tried to solidify a friendship with such a nickname that Matilda suited her just fine, thank you very much. And so, Matilda cultivated a very small group of friends through the years which made her parents begin to question giving their daughter such an adult name, a name their child was now suffering the burden of growing into. They saw the name's liability in every invitation their daughter never received. No surprise birthdays, sleepovers, dances, parties. Their guilt led them to make an appointment with a counselor for Matilda in her senior year. One session later, the counselor asked Matilda to relax in the waiting room while she had a chat with her parents.

The counselor was kind but direct. "Your daughter's name is not her problem. It's yours. Do you know the meaning of her name? She does. It stands for strength. She called it a motto for how she wants to live her life. Did you know that?" The slump of their heads gave the answer. "Matilda is perfectly happy with her life. She admits to being – in her words – 'a little quirky' and is definitely an introvert but happily so on both counts." She completed her analysis of Matilda and then gently suggested they might consider counseling for themselves.

They found Matilda in the waiting room talking quietly in a corner to someone. Her body shielded the stranger until they called her name and she turned. Matilda's mother clutched her husband's hand and dug her fingers into flesh. She willed herself not to gasp. Was this a boy or a man? It was impossible to tell because of the tight web of scars on his face and neck and a trail of ropey flesh that reappeared below his short sleeve and down his right arm. "Mom, Dad, this is Ethan. He goes to my school."

Ethan stood.

Nothing weak about that handshake, Matilda's father registered after awkwardly retracting his right hand to accommodate Ethan's outstretched left one.

Sorry, no right hand," Ethan's apology offered where a greeting would have been.

"Nice to meet you, Ethan. Sorry we have to rush," her father's reply replacing courteous small talk he found impossible to muster. Ethan nodded, used to the response.

"See you tomorrow." Matilda waved as they left.

"Tomorrow."

Matilda's parents managed to get the bones of Ethan's tragic story from Matilda. A house fire. Multiple surgeries and more to come. But that was secondary to why she liked him: his name and how it fit him. First, she liked that he had a name that couldn't be shortened. "A name should stand on its own," Matilda declared. Second, like hers, it meant strong. "Actually, his full name is Tristan Ethan MacNaughton. Tristan means sorrow. He's had a lot of that, but he grew out of that name. Ethan is the perfect fit."

After Matilda went to bed, her parents' conversation roller-coastered from marveling at how much they had learned about their daughter in a single car ride, to chastising themselves for not seeing beyond their own discomfort, to admitting affectionately what an amazing and, yes, even quirky daughter they had.

Weeks later, when Matilda announced that Ethan had invited her to the prom, they were not surprised. They were not surprised when she bucked the trends of silk and spaghetti straps for a modest white dress and black coat so "Ethan and I can be our own raft of penguins in a sea of dancers." They were not surprised when she asked for a bouquet rather than a wrist corsage. Ethan picked roses. He handed her an envelope with a beautiful sketch of Matilda. Inside was a handmade card with a cartoon drawing of Shakespeare and a quote: "A rose by any other name would smell as sweet." Inside was a private note that made her blush.

The surprise came as Matilda's father was taking his final picture of the couple. "Just one of my daughter alone. O.K., Ethan?"

"Sure, Mr. Jeffries. Do you mind if I take one too?" He pulled out his phone. "Smile, Joy."

The name. Joy. Matilda's middle name. Startled, Matilda's father's phone slipped, and his picture captured his daughter, headless, in her penguin finery, roses in one hand, and the card and envelope in the other. Later he would enlarge it to read the message: To Joy. I am glad you have grown into your middle name just like me."

The Tower

James Masciarelli

Garrick stood before the drawbridge, weary but hopeful. Adjusted his girding, then marched thirty steps over the moat risen by spring rains. Will Annora answer the calling bell?

Pondering their arc of friendship, long marriage, and recent events, he pushed through the great arched doors to pull the rope. Three bell strikes echoed atrium colonnades aspersed with tapestries. He held up a candle to light his climb to the far tower. Halfway up, he called her name.

Annora set her paint brush aside, glimpsed out the Romanesque ramparts to a panorama of courtyards, fallow fields, to the sea and back to her canvas.

A card floated to his feet. "Be home by dusk. . . harvest stew with barley bread. Chase me till I catch you."

Somewhat amused, Garrick hiked back to their cottage, built with his strong constitution. His happiness blunted by his lot of dogged pursuit for the great sealed mystery of her heart. He often wondered if her childhood wounds so great, they were unspeakable? She claimed otherwise. . . simply not so complicated as he.

Her mother was a beauty of broken noble ancestry and

failed marriages. Annora's beauty and poise far greater, without the extravagant tastes. At eighteen, Annora had set out on her own without sponsor, property or savings. She rarely spoke of her childhood.

Garrick was no stranger to long marches. He bored easily after each achievement. When obsessed with a new venture, he gave pursuit. Early in their marriage, he would be away for weeks at a time. He treasured Annora's counsel. More than that, she had practical magic.

A master gardener and artist, Annora ran the books, the household and sharpened his focus. They played and worked in the gardens, walled by his stonework terraces suited to her designs. He distracted her from creative passions.

He sighed; I should be the happiest person on Earth. Why does she need to seek refuge somewhere every day? Particularly the Tower. A fortified defense from what?

Let it go, he grumbled. She works her magic behind the scenes, out of the limelight. I yearn her presence. She can live like a cat, and I am all dog. . . an open book to her. She is a great listener. I am an external thinker. Sometimes I need her to process my thoughts and feelings. Without her, I am nothing.

He admired her fortitude and well defended personality from the madness of the world. The advance and retreat of intimacy were like the very seas and tides; but less predictable. It is just her way. She is not a designing woman. But there must be something at work. Unentangled at twenty-nine when they met, she rebuffed all suitors. Indomitable. She spent her youth raising half-sisters and did not want children of her own. Garrick was a young widower with a son he loved dearly. Thankfully Annora embraced them both.

Garrick chuckled. We are perfectionists in our own special ways. I am forever in her web. The only way I could accept my status as "other" during her retreats was to invent the whole notion of the Tower in the first place. With this grand metaphor, I visit loneliness and hope. To the crux of the matter. . . does she need me?

Without hearing those words, I fabricated the Tower to deal with my emotions. But aha. . . it protects us both! I frequent the moat surrounding the castle. That line of defense for the fairest of maidens with an arresting smile of nobility. Tall and light on her feet. Yea.

After all these years, I still do not know. I am a fool. She has her daily retreats and I have her faithful heart.

On the next fine Sunday afternoon, Garrick took Annora for a ride in their convertible and parked on a high bluff overlook to the sea.

He put his arm around her shoulder, looked deep into her eyes and said, "I need you."

He waited.

His lips quivered, "Do you need me?"

"You silly man. Of course I need you, Garrick."

And the walls came tumbling down.

A Safe Place

Dr. Dolores Burton

It had been a long day at the office and she hurried home to take Peanut out for his walk. After all, he hopefully had held it all day. When she opened the door, one envelope was on the floor under the mail slot on the door. She picked it up and was puzzled because it bore no stamp or postmark. She opened it quickly and read the cryptic message, "You are being watched. Be careful." She put the note aside, still puzzled, but Peanut was waiting. She retrieved his leash from the hook near the door and opened the door carefully.

Scanning the street, she paid particular attention to the shadows created by the quickly setting sun. After opening the townhouse door wider, she and her beloved tiny dog Peanut stepped out. As she locked the door behind her, the leaves rustled near the giant oak tree in the front yard. She tried to ignore the noise. There was no wind, so how could the leaves be moving? Peanut, eager to be off, strained at his tiny leash. They walked quickly to the end of the street into the dog park. She felt someone was following her but shrugged it off as being melodramatic.

Due to the late hour, only two other dogs were in the park. Their owners were sitting on the bench near the entrance. She unleashed her dog, and he scampered off to play with the other two dogs near the woods at the far end of the park. Another dog owner threw a ball, and the three puppies ran after it into the woods. It was getting dark and, soon, the owners called their dogs to go home for dinner. Two dogs came running out of the woods and headed home with their owners, but where was Peanut? His owner ran into the woods, and to her horror, Peanut was under a bush lying on the ground. He did not seem injured she picked him up and hurried home. Stepping inside quickly, she closed and locked the door. She sighed in relief. Thank goodness she was in a safe place now, or, was she?

Italian Shoes

Melody Highman

The red door to the Spanish Villa flies open. Mrs. Jones, a shapely woman in spiky heels, clutches a Gucci bag to her bosom. She and her beloved Shihtzu, Chanel, step out into the sunshine. Mrs. Jones casts an askance glance down the street, first left and then right. With sweaty hands she spins around, locks the door and quietly drops the house keys in her bag.

Eager to be off, Chanel, whimpers and tugs on her diamond studded, pink collar. Mrs. Jones and Chanel slink down the paved walkway, veering left at Pampered Pet's Dog Park. As soon as they pass through the gilded gate, Mrs. Jones unleashes Chanel and she pads off, her tail wagging excitedly.

Chanel's favorite bone is tucked inside Mrs. Jones's bag. She decides to wait until the man in Italian shoes arrives before taking it out. Perhaps he will toss the bone to Chanel and she will no longer growl at him.

The sun drops. Mrs. Jones digs the point of her shiny Italian leather stiletto into the dirt and gives it a twist. "Why do I always fall for the married ones?" She mutters under her breath.

Oh! Screw him! She thinks, kicking off her heels and hurling them against the wall of manicured shrubbery, yelling, "Who needs 'em? They hurt my feet anyway!"

"Chanel!" calls Mrs. Jones. "Come girl!"

Barefooted, she secures Chanel's diamond corset and together they strut off along the wooded trail into the sunset.

Patches and Me

Linda Walker

Patches was my dad's truck. A 1974 Ford. 1974 was a bad year for Ford trucks. They rusted out badly. Dad hadn't bought it new, so it already had some miles on it and some rust on it when he got it. As Dad didn't keep it in a garage the rust only got worse. Dad, being an innovative sort of guy, patched up the rusted-out places with small metal sheets used in the printing of our local newspapers, hence the name Patches was dubbed onto the truck by us kids. Dad liked working on vehicles, so he always had more than the one he actually needed. Which resulted in Lough's Loaners as us kids called them. If one of our vehicles was in the shop or out of commission, we borrowed one of Dad's extras.

Being a single working mother at the time I was frequently a borrower as my vehicles were none too roadworthy. One time when I was driving Patches, I heard a terrible noise. I stopped to check and found the right wheel well had completely disintegrated and fallen out into the road. Just a bunch of rust along the road now.

Another time, a lady ran her car into the side of Patches at a red light. Her fault, but my bad as Dad had to spend time calling insurance reps, picking up the police report, and getting estimates. Not a happy time for him or me.

Now that I am around the age my dad was at that time, Patches comes back to my mind. I find I am like Patches in many ways. Patches ran well, gobbled a lot of gas, but he was literally falling apart. So am I. I'm healthy, but sure am beat up. New knees, plate and screws in one arm, shoulder replacement, torn rotator cuff, cataract surgery, a fallen arch. What next? Will something just fall off as I go down this road of old age?

I wish I could remember what became of Patches. Did he just disintegrate in some junk yard? Was he stripped of anything useable? I am a registered organ donor. I'm to be cremated and the cremains spread in the horse pasture. Gone but not forgotten, just like old Patches?

The Apple

Linda Walker

Did this apple fall far from the tree? Was the son like his father? Was the father like his son was more important to me as it was the father who was asking me out.

His son I knew, as he had lived in the neighborhood for several years. I knew he was a rotten apple. I had heard the arguments with his wife ending with him tearing off in his car, not to be seen for a day or so. Then he'd reappear and all would be quiet on the home front for a while. Sooner or later though the neighborhood would witness another go-round. This went on for quite some time until his wife finally had enough and went home to her mother.

Quiet did not follow though. Soon after she left, she was replaced by another woman. Not a wife this time. A live-in. Before long the same scenes were repeated with her. Screaming and cussing and off he'd tear in his car. Only he didn't stay away long. He'd soon be back. A few more battle scenes and then the woman left.

She was followed shortly by another with the same scenes as before played out. I lost count of the number of women who came and went. All leaving after loud confrontations.

Now his mother had died, and his father moved in with him. His mother's death had come after a long, expensive illness and his father had sold his home to pay the medical bills. That was the story told to the neighborhood by the son. He was now taking care of his dad. No more women came to his house.

The father seemed like a nice man. I'd seen him out walking around the neighborhood. He always spoke politely and admired the dogs the neighbors walked. I had seen him pick up the occasional piece of trash which had blown off the garbage truck on trash day. He helped the guy next door when his lawnmower wouldn't start. Like I said, he seemed like a nice man.

But now he had asked me to go out to dinner with him. Just how far from the tree had that apple fallen? Was I willing to risk my heart to someone who had fathered such a son?

A chance run-in with a neighbor answered my question. The neighbor gave me a rundown on the son's history.

Turns out, a gale had blown this apple from the tree. A gale called Desert Storm. The son had joined the Army in order to get an education. Unfortunately, Desert Storm intervened. The education he received in war rotted this apple.

POETRY

AN INTRODUCTION

Poetry embraces us, be it humorous, thoughtful,
stimulating, inspirational.
It is a well–spring of our private
and shared thoughts.

Virginia Read, Board Member at Large
Marco Island Writers Inc.

Waltz

Ryszarda (Lida) Pelc

To my ears melody comes
Slowly, slowly…
Sweet, harmonious, delightful tones surround me
I submerge into the waltz.

Waltz helps me look back to the past.
Waltz takes me to Vienna.

Johan Strauss
Plays in the city park.
Lightness, delicacy of violin.

Bewitchment, charm, fascination.
Vienna. Blue Danube.
World pirouetting in the waltz.

Little Girl From Iowa

Ryszarda (Lida) Pelc

Born in the heart of the country
she never grew up really.
Until now she remembers the tension
around the table at her home in Iowa
and because of that
"I eat only twice a day" she confessed
lying on her back in the Holiday Inn swimming pool.

Mother of three,
lives on the bank of the Le Croix River, in Hudson,
Wisconsin.
When she is done with her daily duties, voluntary
jobs at the hospital
and in the ticket office, with her writing
when she is done with...God knows what else, God
knows what else.

She perches on the balcony watching the white sails
on the river blue, gray, silvery, golden, red or pink,
 depends on the mood of the sky and the density of
the clouds.
She watches walkers, joggers, dogs passing, running
by
and she is longing for her old home in the woods.
Sweet privacy there was nobody around

The girl from Iowa likes beef sandwiches
she has eaten for 25 years in the same restaurant,
nothing ever but beef sandwiches.
She likes silk flowers; red roses and pink tulips which
she bought one day
and decorated her living room with the fireplace and
view...

She has girlfriends.
one of them freezes credit cards in a jar full of salad
dressing.
"This is the best way to avoid spending"
another brought stones, smooth, polished by water.
The girl from Iowa, in her car Le Baron, carries the
stones
in plastic bag, pink ribbon on
and looking at them learns how to make life go
smoothly

This is The End of my story
about girl born in the heart of the country,
about Connie, my friend from Iowa...

Rain Under The Rainbow

Ryszarda (Lida) Pelc

My thoughts wander, wander
under a grayish, cloudy sky.
The weather is like my mood.

Suddenly the heavy rain falls.
It's raining hard,
you say, "it's raining cats and dogs."
We run, we laugh and run.
Cascades of rain on us.

We find shelter under a sugar maple tree.
We listen to the sound of rain.
And then, the rainbow in the sky above us,
and sunshine.

"The purple rain" I whisper bewitched.
We admire the rainbow and the rain.
In beams of the sunset-
the purple rain.

Islander's Confession

Ryszarda (Lida) Pelc

I have to confess my sins.
I am guilty of doing nothing
except walking on the beach crushing under my feet,
dazzling in sun's rays shiny, fragile shells.

I have to confess my guilt of doing nothing
but watching dignified white egrets;
      survivors of evolution, brown pelicans;
      clattery, puffy, arrogant beggars, sea-gulls;
      skimmers and tiny, hasty, amusing sandpipers.

I'm guilty. I do nothing but admire the flying birds
under azure sky, above the emerald mirror of shimmering
waters.

I am guilty of waiting for dolphins, hoping to watch them
while they chase a school of fish, when they play in deep
waters of the Gulf, while they jump high and their dark, wet
bodies reflect the sunbeams.

I confess; I spend hours seating on the beach, I spend hours
seated on the beach,
sifting the white, fine sand through my fingers,
listening to the soothing sound of waves, – reminder of a
long-forgotten sound of water
as listening to while floating safely in my mother's womb
before I was born.

Lake Superior

Ryszarda (Lida) Pelc

Lake Superior
huge, enormous, runs to the horizon, overflows.
Rumbles like a drumbeat of gigantic drums.
Superior…
I'm listening to the roar of the waves,
I'm listening to the whistle of the wind.
I walk through overthrown branches on the shore.

A nostalgia walks with me among the white birch trees.

A roar of waves brings memory of those moments,
which I'm carrying with me through my life and across the
borders.
Memories about the jewel of Adriatic, Ravenna,
where Theodora and Justinian dreams of glory
are expressed in colorful mosaics, the masterpiece of eternal
art.

I recall the busy boulevard in Nice
Facing the blue Mediterranean Sea under the clear sky of the
South.
I save in my memory the beauty of the majestic Pacific Ocean,
misty, mysterious, fascinating, not peaceful at all.

The pictures of those places are alive in my memory.
My heart … My heart belongs to the Baltic,
The sea of my motherland,
Where I first learned how to love the seas.

The Butterfly's Dance

Ryszarda (Lida) Pelc

I saw last summer a butterfly`s dance.
I adored its softness, perfection,
Its finesse.

The colorful butterfly.
Shiny in the beams of sunset,
Tired of dance and daily journey,
Sat on the grass and swung gently,
Swayed by the summer breeze.

The whisper of wildflowers
The buzz of wasps,
The bees drone.
A twitter, chirrup of the flying birds-
Composed the music.
The song of the summer bewitched us,
-the butterfly and me.

"I'm sorry, the day is going to end.
And summer too…"
"And life…" –the butterfly whispered-
He roused
And flew to the sky to dance …once more.

Marco Island never stops surprising with its wonders.
By the intersection of Elkcam Circle and Sixth Avenue.
a Palm Tree shares the root with a Ficus Tree.
Forever.

Journey to Love

Dmitriy Shoutov

Love is hard to find,
More difficult to nurture.
Begins with responsibility.
Can be beauty. Can turn ugly.

Love teases; plays hide and seek.
We get nervous when look for it.
Regardless, we are on the road of
Trials and errors,
Joys and sorrows.

We burn with fire;
Get exhausted, but keep searching.
Quantity turns to quality,
We find the one with whom to Fire Light,
To care about and keep it right.

Art of loving discovered before
Rises to the sky.
Yet, Love slips away.
We call it back
Around and above the Milky-way.

Under same roof we laugh
We cry, we argue, seeking compromise.
Agree together to continue flight.
Eyes promise no more fight.

Without warning,
Body loses power and speed.
We get rid ourselves of sins
We do, or don't commit.

We are confused about Love
Distancing from us.
No goodbye, nor buzz.

We discover youthful joy —
Watching hustles of life,
Having fun when drinking tea
And abstaining from TV.

Reading books together.
Reading each other's minds.
Happiness emits kinds.

Our new acquaintances are
Peace and Harmony.
We missed them badly.

Revelation comes.
True Love
Guided us
Through all the times.

Rhyme Time

Jean Duling

Yes, covid took loved ones. It halted life.
Confinement, so much sickness, pain and strife.

Where did all those active, early days go?
We trudge through fog, wind, rain and snow.

We look to you, oh Lord, to find our way
To walk your path and fill our souls today.

Show us the light, with prayer, song and mirth
This season brings hope: our savior's birth.

Loon Triplet

Jean Duling

Lone loon dives
Surfaces---renewal
New ventures ahead.

Loon yodel echoes
One new birth comes
 In song light.

Loon migrating time
Moments of paradise joy
Yodel Ha-oo-oo.

Tryptych

S. Clay

I

Flexing my muscles.
Pushing boundaries
Seeing your footprints in the snow.
Hearing your fledgling
Clamor & racket.
My shoulders are coiled
Wearing immortality like the
Mighty Hercules or Atlas.
Am I too holding up the world?
You, my worthy creator,
Fashioning any more
Heavenly beings like me.?
A mate perhaps?
My meditation continues,
Covered under the snow
So you know
I am still here
Under wraps."

II

See how I am broken
Quartered, dismembered
My head sits on top of my pelvis
My femur on top of my tibia
My fibula is somewhere out there?
Look at me when you pass
Appealing?
Vacant eyes and a pig-like snout of a nose
My mouth is unbarred
I am speaking to you.
Sorry, no hands to greet you.
No arms to hold you.
Divided and separated
With a hole in my pelvis.
I am a hollow man.
See through me
Empty air is my mind.
I do have curves
Perhaps I am female?
My creator donated me and
Left me here in the Yard
A monument.
Pass me by, but please,
Am I ugly?

III

Am I still beautiful?
Undercover here
Under winter's warmth
Bound and tied up
Stretching against the green plastic.

Flexing my muscles.
Pushing boundaries
Seeing your footprints in the snow.
Hearing your fledgling
Clamor & racket.
My shoulders are coiled
Wearing immortality like the
Mighty Hercules or Atlas.
Am I too holding up the world?
You, my worthy creator,
Fashioning any more
Heavenly beings like me.?
A mate perhaps?
My meditation continues,
Covered under the snow
So you know
I am still here
Under wraps."

"Though you are no longer with us, you will never be forgotten. May your memory be forever held in the pages of this book."

Author Unknown

Marco Island Writers Inc. most likely would not exist without the support and input we received from these six members who have passed away. Each brought something unique and different to the table. Each are sincerely missed.

We have included three of these authors excerpts from one of their published works. We honor author's copyrights and could only use excerpts where we received written authorization from the heirs. All six are included in our About the Authors section.

Joanne Tailele, President, Marco Island Writers Inc.

Excerpt from Out of Hong Kong

Vince D'Angelo

By late afternoon his interest in the Chinese districts was satisfied. Thinking about what to do next, Bradshaw's third card came to mind. Going through his pockets, he found it.

Bradshaw had written: The Royal Stock Traders Lodge, including its address.

Why would Bradshaw recommend such a place? He knows Doyle and I aren't investors. Why spend time in those stodgy British men's clubs I've seen in movies? But he hasn't steered us wrong yet and it's too early for Doyle and Chan to return so I might as well give it a try.

He hailed a taxi and showed the driver the address Bradshaw had written on the back of the card. The driver nodded and smiled. He seemed familiar with the place. The driver sped off with the same reckless abandon as Chan and drove into the quieted Central District, then turned into a side street where a row of English-Tudor style buildings was located. Signs on the doors indicated the buildings were business and professional offices closed for the Sunday. The taxi stopped in front of one.

There was a large, dark-stained wood door displaying an ornate wood-carved shield. In the middle of the shield was inscribed, The Royal Stock Traders Lodge, flanked by two lion images. Below the shield was a sign that read: Members Only. Hayes hesitated before getting out of the taxi.

I should wait until I'm with Doyle.

I've time to kill, so why not?

He paid the driver and stepped out of the taxi. He walked a few steps, then turned to tell the driver to wait until he had a chance to check the place out. The driver had made the decision for him. He'd left! Hayes was irritated because it was not one of those streets where taxis came by frequently on a Sunday.

On the door, above the shield, was an iron doorknocker. He knocked and waited. No one responded. He was about to leave when a small door above the knocker opened. The opening was only large enough for him to see an Asian man's eyes peering out, looking at him. It reminded Hayes of one of the gangster movies where the person who knocked would say, "Joe sent me."

An impassive sounding voice with a Chinese accent asked, "Can I help you?"

"I was recommended to, ah, come by," answered Hayes.

"This is a membership club and only accepts guests when accompanied by a member."

"Oh, I see," Hayes said. "But I was told by . . ." The little door shut. He turned and walked away, annoyed he hadn't retained the taxi.

This leaves me stuck here. It doesn't seem like a place I'd be interested in any way. But it puzzles me why Bradshaw recommended it. He must have had a reason.

Recalling how Bradshaw's cards had opened doors before, he turned back and knocked on the door again. When the little door opened, he held Bradshaw's business card close in front of it.

The little door closed and the large door opened. Holding the door open was a robust, well-groomed, Chinese man looking to be in his forty's, wearing a black suit, white shirt, and narrow black tie. His black hair was slicked back tight into a short queue. As Hayes entered, the man quickly closed the door behind him. "Welcome sir," the man said cordially. Hayes held out his hand and quickly withdrew it, recalling it was not the Chinese custom to shake hands and just uttered, "Thank you."

"You are most welcome, sir," said the man in a tone that sounded to Hayes to be more procedural than sincere. Hayes looked around. They were in a small foyer with wood paneled-walls, no furniture, two wall lamps and an Oriental rug. To Hayes, its starkness belied the pretentious name.

"I am the manager and will shortly put you with our concierge," the man said in articulate, Chinese-accented English. "Please let me have the card and one thousand dollars, Hong Kong."

It was about half the money Hayes had on him. Even in Hong Kong dollars, he felt it was a pretty stiff guest fee.

The manager counted the money and put it in a wall safe he'd quickly opened and shut with a clang that seemed to be a signal; a door on the far side of the foyer opened. A man who closely resembled and was similarly attired as the manager stepped inside. "I am the concierge, sir. Please follow me."

He followed the concierge person out through the doorway. Instead of walking into a large drawing room filled with cigar and pipe-smoking, stodgy old British men reading newspapers, exchanging investment information and sipping brandy, he was walking down a carpeted, dimly lit hallway.

He noticed there were a number of uniformly spaced doors along both sides of the hallway. It was spotlessly clean and fresh smelling, yet no maids or any other persons were about. He heard sounds and occasional muffled voices coming from the doors they passed.

Each door had a small light fixture on the wall next to it. Some of the lights were lit, others weren't. It didn't seem like a place that would leave light bulbs burned out. It gave the appearance of a hotel, except that the doors weren't numbered.

Hayes tried to figure out what the place was all about.

Though it gave the appearance of a hotel, no request was made for him to sign a registry or even his name asked. It suddenly dawned on him!

The place is a brothel!

He started to move up close to the concierge to tell him he wished to leave, but his curiosity was piqued. He'd never been in a brothel before. His youthful inquisitiveness wanted to be satisfied. A tingling sensation of adventure came over him. His mother's image suddenly flashed before him. The admonition she had given him before he left home for the Navy, reverberated in his mind: "Always conduct yourself as if you were in the presence of your family."

Don't worry Mom; no one can make me do anything I don't want to. I just want to have a look.

Her image was quickly dispelled by his growing curiosity.

The hallway ended at a facing door. The concierge opened the door with a key and stood aside to allow Hayes to enter into a small vestibule. The concierge locked the first door and then unlocked the second door and held it open for him.

Hayes stepped into a room where a number of young Chinese girls sat in pairs at small round tables, talking, sipping tea. The girls were all very pretty, wearing judicious makeup, their long shiny, straight black hair cascading down their backs. They wore the traditional Chinese cheongsams in various colors and designs, which looked to be of higher quality than those worn by the Wan Chai girls, and high-heeled shoes. With his and the concierge's entry, their conversations hushed and teacups were set down. The girls looked over at them smiling prettily and seductively.

On a far wall were two sets of tall, yellow curtains on the sides of windows that were only painted on the wall. Large, illuminated, round paper lanterns hung from the ceiling, putting a warm glow on everything and everyone.

The concierge ushered Hayes to a table which held two sets of teacups and saucers edged with gold, ornamental Oriental design, white napkins, silver spoons and sugar cubes in a small bowl.

Against a far wall was a stand holding an electric hotplate with a steaming teapot on it. One of the girls came over with a tea decanter. Hayes was going to decline but recalled serving tea to a guest was a Chinese welcoming custom.

Bradshaw's offhand comment that tearooms could be very satisfying places came to his mind.

Hayes and the concierge quietly sipped their tea. He was unsure of what was expected of him. However, the girls' continual glances and smiles directed at him, left no doubt: He was to select one of the girls. The girls were all very similar looking, all very attractive and mannequin-like. He wasn't yet sure he wanted to continue on.

I can leave any time I wish. I feel I've already gotten my money's worth!

As they were quietly finishing their tea the concierge asked, "Is there any young lady you fancy?"

This is like being a kid in a candy store.

One young lady he hadn't noticed before caught his eye. She was seated alone at a table in a far corner, not joining the other girls in the ritualistic glancing and smiling. She wore office-girl clothes, a dark skirt with a white blouse and low-heeled shoes, looking more like one of the Chinese girls who worked in the Central District offices. She wore no makeup but was still very attractive. Her black hair was in a ponytail that fell well down her back. She appeared to be detached from the rest and from what was going on, and younger than the others.

Being she's dressed differently than the others she might

not be one I could select. I'll be disappointed because I relate to her more than any of the others. She looks more natural.

The concierge noticed him looking at her. "I believe you have made your choice, sir?"

"Ah-h, yes. I…ah…suppose so," Hayes stammered.

"I will escort you to your room, sir."

As he and the concierge rose to leave, the girls withdrew their glances and smiles and returned to their chatting and tea sipping.

Hayes followed the concierge down the quiet hallway. Again, no one was in sight, and there were only the sounds of voices coming from some of the rooms. It was obvious everything was well-orchestrated to maintain the utmost of privacy for the 'guests.'

The concierge stopped at one of the doors, opened it with a key, reached inside and snapped on a light-switch as he held the door open for him. Hayes noticed the unlit light fixture on the hallway wall next to the door had lit. He understood the reason why some of the hallway fixtures next to the doors were lighted and others weren't. The switch had also turned on a dim lamp on a gray-painted, wood table alongside a bed, and a slowly turning, overhead ceiling fan.

The concierge stepped aside and motioned him to enter. As they walked in the carpeted room the door quietly closed itself.

The room had a clean appearance and odor. The bed had a plain gray comforter. A crisp white sheet showed from under it. There were two large, white pillows at the head of the bed. A similar table on the other side of the bed held a plain black phone that had no dial, and a glass ashtray. The walls and ceiling were painted in gray.

A gray, leather, stuffed chair was in a far corner. In the opposite corner, an open door revealed a small lavatory with a high window. The only window. The gray-themed room was decorated and furnished sparsely, but appropriately, for its purpose.

The concierge watched as Hayes looked about the room and in the same ritual voice, asked, "Is everything to your satisfaction, sir?"

"Huh? Oh, ah, yes," Hayes mumbled.

"The young lady will come by shortly to visit with you. Make yourself comfortable." At that, the concierge turned and left the room.

Comfortable? I've never felt so out of place my entire life.

Once again, his mother's visage flashed before him. It was quickly replaced by the image of the young, pretty girl he believed he'd selected.

Hayes took off his shoes and lay down on the bed. The familiar act of lying on a bed with his shoes off, his head on a pillow with his hands under his head put him at ease. He was further comforted thinking once again that though he had gone along with everything so far, he didn't have to go through with anything he didn't want to do. He made up his mind to just deal with things as they came along, just as he'd been doing. He waited in pleasant anticipation for the girl, anxious to be in her company.

Staring up at the slowly turning ceiling fan had a mesmerizing effect on him, relaxing him, making him forget for the moment where he was.

"Sir?" a girl's soft voice came from the corner near the door.

He bolted upright. The light from the table lamp revealed it was the girl he hoped he'd selected. The composure he had been enjoying left him. He could only manage a nervous, "Hello," as he jumped up and stood next to the bed and looked at her.

Her pale luminous skin accentuated her brown, almond-shaped eyes, long arching eyebrows, and red lips. The girl's ponytail had been unfurled and her hair hung long and straight down her back. She was very beautiful. She wore the same office-girl attire, which he had liked, something more familiar to him than the cheongsam dresses the other girls in the tearoom wore. Once again, he wasn't sure what to say or do.

The girl appeared to be waiting for his instructions. "How are you, sir?" she said, breaking the awkward silence.

"Ah, fine, thanks. Would you like to, ah, sit down?" He held his hand out in the direction of the large stuffed chair in the corner. As she walked across the room she seemed to be walking somewhat awkwardly. He saw she was now wearing high-heeled shoes.

She sat upright and straight-backed on the edge of the chair, revealing a pair of shapely legs. The largeness of the chair made her appear even more petite.

What am I supposed to do now? I've never been in a brothel before! And don't really want to be! I'll just think of this place as an escort service and ask her if she'd like to go some-where for dinner.

His fantasy was interrupted. "You are American, sir?"

"Oh yes, American…very American."

"I like Americans. They are very nice."

Hayes found her soft, Chinese-accented voice captivating. Her compliment, whether sincere or routine, calmed him. He sat down on the edge of the bed facing her, trying to act as if he was experienced at this sort of thing and continued his delusion that she was a paid escort rather than a prostitute. He wouldn't mind if they just spent their time together just talking. He was curious to know what she was all about, how such a young girl came to be in this kind of a place.

They remained quiet for a few long moments, looking at each other. Her with a gentle smile. Him, dumb-struck and ex-pressionless, trying to think of something to say. He was about to ask for her name.

But no one else here has used a name. But she did ask my nationality so I should be entitled to ask her the same.

"Where are you from, ah, Miss?"

"Hong Kong."

Foolish question. What else would a person in her position say?

After another uncomfortable silence and staring, she rose from the chair and walked over to him, took him by surprise, hugging him around the neck and kissing him gently on the mouth. They fell backward onto the bed, locked in her kiss and embrace. The tenderness of her kiss gave him the feeling it was sincere. Absurd, but it made him feel good. He wrapped an arm firmly around her waist, which was so small his arm reached around her and his hand touched his own waist. He pulled her tightly against himself. Her warm supple body pressed against his gave him sensations of arousal. When their lips separated they lay side-by-side with their heads on the pillows, their faces only inches apart. They were both breathing heavily, staring into each other's eyes, with their arms still entwined around each other.

He found himself under the spell of the stunning girl, and so pleased, he pondered about how much time they could spend together. Something neither the concierge nor the man-ager had mentioned.

"How much time do we get to be together?"

"As long as you wish, sir."

Addressing him as 'sir' brought him back the reality that he was just another client to her. He supposed there'd be additional charges the longer he stayed. It wasn't about the money. He just wanted to be with the captivating girl as long as possible.

He couldn't believe or understand his feelings for her after being together for only a little time and under such circumstances. He'd often heard of love-at-first-sight.

But with a prostitute in a brothel?

His silent contemplation must have puzzled her. The gentle smile left her face and she sat up. Looking down at him with a concerned look she asked, "Are you happy, sir?" "Would you like me to leave and you can choose another girl?"

"Oh, no, no! You're wonderful. Absolutely wonderful!" he blurted out. His fervent declaration returned her smile and a small giggle. He figured she was amused by his outburst, but he didn't care. He was glad he had pleased her. She lay back down and once again their heads were on the pillows facing each other. Their new-found casualness encouraged him to ask, "My name is Hayes. What is yours?"

She said nothing and just continued the smile. They stayed in the same position, lying on the bed in a loose embrace, silently looking into each other's eyes.

"Why did you choose me?" she asked.

"Because, well, because you stood out."

"Why I stood out?"

"I guess I related to you more than the other girls. You weren't wearing one of those fancy dresses the other girls wore and were without all the make-up. You were dressed more like the girls back home. Besides, you're prettier than the others!"

Her smile broadened and a merry look came to her eyes. Then her demeanor changed to somber.

"I work in the office of a British company. Here I must dress like the other girls. I did not have time to change when I came today."

"You mean you're working two jobs?"

"No. I will work only here if they want me."

"Want you?"

"Yes. The British men will tell them if I can stay."

"British men run this place?"

Her brow pinched. Her look became one of worry. "I can say no more. I have said too much. I can have trouble."

This is obviously a place where well-to-do British men can discreetly do their thing. Hiding it under the pretext of being an investment house where their wives would have no reason to come.

She sat up as if she had suddenly thought of something. He sat up and she began to unbutton his shirt.

"I can do that," he said and pulled her hands away.

"If you wish, sir," she said in a disappointed sounding voice.

Her trying to unbutton his shirt brought back the troubling realization she was a prostitute in a brothel. What he had tried not to believe.

Why doesn't she just work for the British company? It's far more respectable. What is she doing in this place?

She got up from the bed and stood alongside it, facing him with closed eyes and a dispassionate expression, and unbuttoned her blouse revealing a red brassiere over small, extended breasts. Removing the blouse she let it fall to the floor.

She unhooked her skirt and let it drop down around her feet clad in the high-heeled shoes. She was wearing red panties that matched her brassiere.

She stood motionless with her arms hanging down her sides as if to allow him to examine her scantily-clad body. Her eyes opened with a strange inexplicable look.

The sight of her took his breath away. It was something he had never before seen. He stood up and quickly began unbuttoning his shirt and tossed it aside, removed his trousers and tossed them aside. He was so excited he was barely breathing. He stood there in his shorts that were extended out in front by his visceral reaction to the sight of her. He reached out, took her by the waist and lifted her off the floor so their faces were at the same level, and pulled her tight against him and gave her a lingering kiss. There was no return kiss.

She suddenly became limp in his arms. Her body arched back away from his. Her expressionless face was turned upward with its eyes closed. Hayes thought she had fainted.

Suddenly, her entire body began shaking. Her arms rose, her hands covered her face and she began sobbing.

Did I do something wrong? Was it because she saw how he scantily-clad body had affected me? It couldn't be something new to a girl in her position!

He drew her slumped body back against him and held her head so the side of her face was against his chest. He felt tears running down. He picked her up bodily, placed her on the bed, lay down next to her and pulled her tightly to him. She didn't react in any way. As though she had submitted herself completely to him, to do with her as he wished.

Their heads were once again on the pillows facing each other, her eyes still closed. He gently stroked her hair, pushing strands from the tear-stained face.

"What is the matter?" he asked.

She didn't answer. After a minute had passed her expressionless face opened its eyes. Still, she said nothing, just stared at him.

His curiosity became intense. "Please! Tell me what's wrong. Did I do something to offend you?"

After a few moments, she said, "My name is Su Yin."

He was surprised and stunned she had given her name.

"Su Yin? It's a very pretty name." He paused. "Su Yin, what happened to you and why did you cry and react the way you did?"

She put her head against his chest, said nothing, and wrapped her arms around him which greatly relieved and pleased him. She was quiet for a while and then said, "You are not the reason I cry. I am the reason I cry."

Hayes was thankful he wasn't to blame, but her answer puzzled him.

"I cry because…because I have never done this before."

"You haven't done what before?" said Hayes, bewildered.

"I have never been a. . .prostitute before," she said firmly.

"But you work in this place. . . ."

"I told you! Never!" Her voice was adamant.

He could feel her heart pounding against his chest. He put his hand under her chin, raised her head and looked at her. "Su Yin, I really don't understand!"

"You are my first, the very first one."

"Your first. . . ? But you seemed to know exactly what you were doing, wanting to take off my clothes, kissing me, undressing. . . ."

"They teach me."

"Who taught you?"

"The other girls. They teach me what to do."

He wanted to believe what she told him but had trouble with it.

They lay there quietly, still in the embrace. Hayes was still mystified by what she had told him, trying to make sense of it all.

"I am very sad about it, sad about what I am doing," she said softly.

"Then why are you doing it?" he asked.

She pushed herself away from him and looked at him with an anguished look. "I must do it. I need to do it," she hissed.

"Su Yin, I didn't mean to . . ."

"I do it because. . ." She fell back against him with her head once again on his chest. He took her arms and put them back around him.

She spoke without moving her head from his chest. "My mother and father are in China." Her body began to tremble. "It is very bad for them." She paused. "It takes much money to get them out. I cannot do it working in a British company office!"

I'd like to believe her. I want very much to believe her! But did the other girls also teach her to say such things to extract more money from their clients?

"I am sorry. I should not tell you my troubles."

"No, no, it's okay, it's okay, Su Yin." He sensed he was already involved…in some way or another.

They remained entwined in each other's arms.

He had developed strong feelings for the girl. He knew he was vulnerable because it was his first time in the privacy of a room, on a bed with a beautiful, near-naked young girl.

"I believe you, that I am your first." He hesitated. "I know I shouldn't be asking this. I was wondering if. . . ?"

"I have never been with a man before. My parents were very strict.

Although appalled by her circumstance, he couldn't help but chuckle inwardly.

Seems like I'm not the only virgin in the room.

She felt his chest moving and looked up at him with a curious expression.

"It's nothing, nothing really," he explained, feeling guilty for making light of such a serious matter. She put her head back against his chest and they put their arms around each other once again.

He was trying to sort it all out. He wanted to get her out of there before she really did become a prostitute. But he was still suspicious it was something she'd been coached to say.

I want to help her, but I have to be sure she's sincere. That it isn't just a money ploy. I have an idea, a way to find out.

"I can feel you are thinking very much," she said.

"Su Yin! My family has money. I'll give you some right now, and more money very soon. You'll be able to leave here and have enough money to. . . ."

She broke out of the embrace, pushed herself away and glared at him. "I would not do such a thing. I would not take money from a stranger I did not deserve! I would not do it!" She put her face down on the pillow and cried softly.

Hayes had found out what he wanted to know.

She turned over onto her back and reached for his hand and held it. Gazing up at the ceiling, she began to speak. "I lived in a small village. My father and mother were the teachers. I was their only child. Father taught us English. He said it was important to learn English. When the people of the new government found out they dismissed them. They had to do very hard work in the fields. My parents hid me in a farm truck that was coming here to Hong Kong. Father had been correct. Speaking English let me to work in a Hong Kong British office. Pay is little. It will take much money to get mother and father out of China before they are worked to death. Working here is the only way for me to do it."

"I'm going to get you out of here, Su Yin. I don't know how, but I'll figure something out."

She sat up abruptly. There was a frightened look on her face. "You cannot! I must make the money I need."

Her reaction startled him. "But I want to help you, Su Yin!"

"You cannot help me. You must stop this talk."

They both fell back on the bed looking straight up, not speaking. She pushed away his hands when he tried to hold her. The feelings of arousal had left him, replaced by amorous, protective feelings for this beautiful, troubled girl.

I've got to find a way to take her away from this place. Then I can help her. My family has the financial resources. But first I need to convince her to trust me.

"Su Yin. . ."

"Please, do not try to help. It will only make trouble. I need to do what I must do."

Hayes marveled at how someone so young could believe so strongly in herself, know what she wanted and what she had to do to get it.

"Listen to what I have to say, please," he pleaded.

She turned away from him.

He reached over and pulled her back facing him. "Here's what we can do." He waited to see if she showed interest in what he was about to say. Her eyes were closed her brow pinched. "You must get out of this place. Out of Hong Kong and go to America."

Her eyes flared open and glared at him. "Go to America? Crazy talk!"

Despite her response, he persisted. "An American dollar is worth five to seven Hong Kong dollars. Working in America you will be earning money faster."

Her head lurched back, she gave him a look of disdain. "You want me to be prostitute in America?"

He was initially amused by her misconception. "Of course not! In America, you can get a good job. You speak good English and fluent Chinese. You could work for one of the many Chinese import and export companies. You'll make good money and get your parents out of China even sooner."

Her wary look dissolved into an appreciative smile. She reached out and gently touched his face. "You are a good man, Hayes," she said softly.

He was buoyed by her remembering his name and what she said, believing it to be a sign she had the same feelings for him as he had for her and would go along with his plan. But he hadn't yet a plan to get her out of there and needed to come up with one. He wanted to get it through to her that he was seriously intent on finding a way to get her out of there.

"Su Yin, do you have a passport?" Her puzzled look told him she probably didn't know what one was. "Could you get one?"

She didn't answer.

Pondering over it a bit longer, he recalled many American sailors had married Filipino girls. He could see no reason why he couldn't marry a Chinese girl. He put his face above hers. "Once

I get you out of here we could get married! Then I would be allowed to have you sent stateside."

She drew her head back and glared at him. "You are getting more crazy!"

"I'm serious!" he said emphatically.

They both fell back onto the bed looking upward and became quiet.

Did I just propose to a prostitute in a brothel? But she isn't one and won't be one if I can help it. My family would be in shock learning about my marrying a native Chinese girl. But she's been well-schooled. Mom would surely like that. I wouldn't tell them how I met her. Once they got to know her, they'd love her too.

The first obstacle to his plan would be to get her to believe he was sincere and convince her he would find a workable plan. He wondered how much hold the people who ran the place had on her. The person who could help him get her out of there was Bradshaw! He had all the right connections. With that in mind, he asked, "When we leave here, where . . . ?"

"We cannot leave here together," she hissed. "They do not allow it."

"Then where are you going when you leave here?"

"If they tell me they want me, I will go back to my room to pick up my belongings and bring them here where I will stay, where all the girls who work here stay."

"Good!" said Hayes. "It means when you leave to get your stuff, I'll take you to stay somewhere else."

She shook her head vigorously. "No, No! A man will come with me and help get my things and bring them here. Please! Do not make trouble," she said with tremor in her voice.

"I guess I need to give it some more thought."

They laid back down holding hands.

"I like you want to help me. I want to leave here and go with you. But it is not possible."

Despite everything she said, he was undeterred.

"Su Yin?"

"Yes?" she whispered in a suspicious tone of voice.

"When will you be going to your place?"

"Stop!" she said in the tremoring voice. "You will make only trouble." Her voice softened, "I want to go to America. But it cannot be. It cannot be!"

Introspection – The Key
from The Ochre Hand

Don Erdek

In each of us there is something special.
At the creation of the universe, there was a special something.
It is what religions seek to find.

A belief in something greater, something special.
Something more than the universe itself.
Seeking that something special must be done one life-
time at a time.

Not words enough to explain not thought enough to expend.
Not understanding enough for one with but a frail yet al-
mighty existence.
The individual realizes his true nature only by bringing self into
harmony with the universal purpose.

Above all know thyself, know how thou does think.
The key to real freedom is introspection.
Sense perception and reason can give us knowledge of the
world of physical things.
However the higher realm of the spiritual is of such difficulty
that only a few accede.
If you don't know yourself, if you don't rely on your own judg-
ments, you've wasted a lifetime.
Take time to think.
Everyone should take time to think - so few do.
Time to think is quiet time - time alone.
Not many allow themselves this privilege - this passage
to true freedom.
A freedom to trust oneself and one's own judgments.
To avoid being a clone of someone else or a composite of many.

How does one find oneself if not alone - by oneself?
When others are around it is too easy to become a part of the group
rather than an entity of self. Others seldom let you be - simply you.
Truth is if you don't give yourself time to think you will be unable
to find yourself.
Thinking is something you can neither buy nor sell.

So do you think or do you merely repeat what you heard
someone else say?
Do you think or merely regurgitate what you heard on
the evening news?
Are your morals and ethics defined lock, stock and barrel by
some politician, pundit, priest, religious leader with little of
your own critique?
Is the media and their monomaniacal, self-serving talking heads
your enlightenment - your source for knowledge and truths?
That's not thinking - that's listening!

How many never move beyond being told how to live as well
as what, when, and how to think? Do many take more than
an instant to answer a question and not much more to decide
pro-choice or not?
Or to enter some silly, inane debate about whether or not women
should be allowed in combat. As if war is not the true issue for
mankind's resolution.
Is deep thought avoided as a waste of time? Is all opinion shunted
to cyberspace?
And is cyberspace mostly a forward and seldom a new?
So let me provide you a first guide.
Take more time for your conscience, your soul, to provide direction.
Linger there a little longer and take time to recall those memories
and knowledge you stored for future time.
Well, the future is in the here and now, whether you know it or
not, or even like it or not.
Take time enough to analyze and judge.
That in it may be wisdom enough.

A Lantern Guides a Rite of Passage
from The Ochre Hand

Don Erdek

It was a long time ago for I am an old man now.

My mind's eye can still see the Coleman lantern's orange-white light sitting in the middle of an oversized table.

Huddled around and mesmerized by the lamp's glow are six cocoon-like figures.

Six young Boy Scouts sit Indian style atop a rough-hued table, each drawing strength from the nearness, seeking composure, from the comradery and a lantern.

Only the oval of faces peered out from sleeping bag encased bodies reveal the existence of life.

The lantern's steady light and soft energy their eyes only focus.

That long-ago January night was the first of three wilderness tests to be passed, alone without adult supervision, to enter a new order of scouting, the Sons of Hiawatha.

The day passed bitter cold, the requirements to hike, track, cook outdoors, and find a specific camp location were successfully done.

Constructing a log bridge across a swollen waterway the only real challenge.

Sub-zero daytime temperatures plunged lower as night approached and the wind's howl and moan was in lockstep with the night's dark-fall.

The day's ten-mile trek into the mountains and through a craggy gorge ended at this remote Boy Scout nature lodge which normally is used only for summer excursions.

The lodge was not reached until dusk.

The interior of the lodge provided adequate shelter even with the many strong drafts entering from between the unsealed logs.

Upon arrival the scouts each selected and settled in on the

several bunk beds that were built along a far wall.

But almost in unison they abandoned the bunks for that wooden table.

Although the cabin was shelter from the howling wind and bitter cold it created its own form of apprehension.

On the shelves were animal skulls surrounded by an array of bare bleached white bones, there were countless formaldehyde filled jars with rattlesnakes, salamanders, spiders and tadpoles floating grotesquely within, a mounted raccoon greedily grabbing for something in the open air, a bobcat silently snarled showing a full mouth of sharp teeth, a she wolf protecting her pups, but most ominous was that five-foot wing-spanned vulture with beady red piercing eyes swooping down from the ceiling right above the door to the outside.

The first hour of that evening they discussed their tasks and shared an elation in being alone, in control, and pride in their accomplishments.

However not one of the boys was eager to leave the group and go to bed.

None admitted to the slow creep of anxiety.

Anxiety created by the solitude and remoteness of the location heightened by the frigid-cold outside and wailing wind.

Anxiety soon turned to fear of those many hideous wide-open eyes peering intently from the bottles, from the ghastly and ghostly animals stationed at each corner of the room and especially from the vulture hanging just above their heads guarding the exit door.

So they had sought companionship and gathered around that central table.

Uneasy talk became a silence as slowly, one by one, each abandoned the benches to climb up on the table and be closer to the glow and succor of the lantern.

The day's youthful elation had become a creeping anxiety which then overcame them with fears of the night.

The sentinel lantern kept watch over the silence, its glow softened the fears, finally dimming the lids into drowsy sleep.

And when morning dawned none could recall how long the orange glow continued. Each knew it lasted longer than they did and had become the guide and light to cross that rite of passage.

Excerpt from Deadly News

Don Farmer

PARK TOWERS, BUCKHEAD - ATLANTA

"What the hell was that?" Jody Portier said out loud. He was sitting on the roof of his live truck, sweating, as he fiddled with the faulty microwave dish he had just removed from the pole atop the truck.

He felt the truck rock, then a warm, wet splat on the top of his head.

"Christ, what..." Jody's upward glance froze in shock as he a got another splash of that wet stuff full in the face. He wiped his eyes and wished he hadn't.

Jody was a Global News Service engineer whose TV remote truck was parked in the half-circle driveway at the lobby of the Park Towers.

He had been trying to fix the dish and had taken it off the mast, an extendible metal pole.

Jody had just raised the mast to thirty feet, so the other engineer inside the truck could see whether the problem with their test signal was in the mast cables.

The mast elevated the microwave dish to send audio and video signals to the GNS receiver atop its building downtown.

The GNS news team was there to do a "live shot," a live remote broadcast from the party for Bren Forrest in the condo forty-six floors above.

Miller Andrews, the news cameraman working with Jody, was standing at the rear doors of the truck, getting a battery and a spare P2 digital memory card for his video camera.

He also felt the truck shudder and looked up to see what it was.

"Oh god, oh god, Jody are you OK? Jesus, Jody, there's... oh God, look at that!"

Miller grabbed his camera and began to shoot video. Mentally he was on autopilot, the same way he had reacted in tense situations before, in Fallujah a lifetime ago, in the big earthquake in Haiti and in other "oh crap" situations during his years as a TV news photographer.

With all that experience - the eternal Arab-Israeli carnage, a couple of plane crash aftermath scenes, the Mexican drug wars - Miller had never seen what he saw when he felt that jolt and looked up at the roof of the TV truck.

Staring back at him, the eyes open in surprise and frozen in death, was a man, his arms outstretched, his hands open as if anticipating a bear hug.

The legs were spread-eagled, too, and Miller's shocked mind saw the whole picture as a sort of human wind chime, suspended in air.

Then Miller saw why. The man was impaled on the mast atop the TV truck. He had fallen face down. The square metal cap on the top of the pole had punctured his chest. The mast protruded about three feet out of his back.

Jody was trying to stand up on the roof, staggering, wiping the blood from his eyes.

Miller was dizzy for a moment as his video camera recorded the scene. His shock abated as he squinted through the viewfinder.

He zoomed his lens back to get a wider view, showing the entire body of the man, the mast holding him up there as blood oozed and dripped down the pole and puddled on the truck's roof.

GNS HEADQUARTERS

Max was standing by the domestic assignment desk, talking with a writer for the GNS live broadcast, when the phone rang next to him.

"News, Jackson speaking," said the writer.

Silence. Jackson listened, nodded and listened some more. Then he hung up, his hand shaking.

"What, what?" said Max, exasperated at Jackson's silence.

"Holy shit," Yusef Jackson said.

"What is it?" Max asked again.

"Somebody just landed on the mast of our live truck."

"What do you mean, landed?" Max said.

"No shit! The tech called from the truck over at the Carrier party, at Park Towers. He says the mast on top of the van was fully extended and a body just came outta nowhere and spiked itself on the mast!"

PARK TOWERS

Cassie opened the door of the news van with the station logo all over it before Daryl had completely stopped. As her feet hit the pavement, she saw lights go on around the Global News Service live truck. She turned on her cell and yelled into it as she ran.

A news crew from another Atlanta TV station, arriving to cover the party, also saw the GNS camera lights go on. The news photog walked over quickly to where Miller was recording video.

"Chuck, Cassie here, we gotta go live Chuck, some guy just fell outta the building onto a TV truck. He's dead, I guess," she panted as she caught her breath next to Miller. Her own cameraman, Daryl, ran up behind her and began shooting video of the impaled body.

"Yeah, at the Carrier's building, the big party. What do you mean we can't interrupt regular programming?" Cassandra shouted into the phone.

"For godssake, Chuck, somebody falls out of the building where every VIP in town is attending a party and we can't take it live?"

Cassandra's voice got louder as she caught her breath.

"Who is he? Whattaya mean who is he?" she snapped. "What the hell difference does it make who he is? He's a dead guy. Ever see a guy skewered on a TV truck mast, Chuck? It's a first, godammit, so let's go live in a coupla minutes.

"Oh for...jeez, Chuck I don't know how... that's...just get us on, now!"

Cassandra's mocha complexion was reddening now, sweat trickling down her temples. Her black hair was matted with humidity and sweat from the heat of the July night and the run-around tension of the moment.

"Can you believe this jerk on the assignment desk?" she huffed to Daryl, as he continued to shoot the scene unfolding before him.

"He says we normally don't report suicides, so Chuckie has to call the boss at home for permission to break in."

Daryl laughed but kept recording, walking backwards to get an extra wide shot and a pan down from the building to the speared body.

The security guard from the front desk of the building saw the two camera lights and sauntered out of the glass door into the driveway.

"What's up guys?"

"Up there," Miller motioned with his head.

The guard looked up, saw the body on the mast and saw Jody now sitting cross-legged on the roof of the truck, wiping blood off his face and clothes, silent, disbelief slowing his motion.

The security man looked sick. Miller thought he might collapse and shouted, "Call the cops."

The security man recovered and walked haltingly back into the lobby. At that point two police cars screamed to a stop out front. One officer got on his cell phone and the other began asking rapid-fire questions of the stunned security guard.

Another TV truck drove up at that point, with the blazing words "News9NOW Mobile Bureau," front, back and on both sides. The station had three of those video vans, but the promotions department renamed them mobile bureaus shortly after the station closed its real bureaus in the outlying small cities of Athens, Rome and Peachtree City. It saved money.

A reporter with salt and pepper hair - he had added the pepper - jumped out of the truck and jogged to the officer on the cell phone.

The channel 9 photographer went to where the others were shooting.

"Who's that?" he asked. The newsies all shrugged and kept recording.

"It can't be who I think it is, can it?" the cameraman asked. More shrugs.

A squad car arrived, then another, then an ambulance, lights flashing, and three uniformed officers rushed up.

A sergeant on a cell phone was heard saying,

"Alert the chief."

"He's there, at the party? Go up and tell him."

"No, I don't want to go up there. Can't you text him?

"Damn. Stand by."

The sergeant directed a patrolman to put up some yellow crime scene tape and get the media back behind it.

Detective Hagan slid his car behind one of the squad cars and walked over to talk with the sergeant. Jimmy then looked around, hoping to spot Cassie. He heard her first, talking animatedly on her cell.

I'll have to tease her about pushing that guy off the balcony just so she'd have a big crime story to report tonight. Nah, better not. She might push me outta bed instead.

Jimmy walked into the lobby and to the bank of elevators.

If this turns out to be a homicide, it could be a long night for me. And Cassie too, but not with each other.

At that moment, Sheila Belle, the GNS entertainment reporter who was there to do the live report on the festivities, walked from the ladies' room in the lobby out to the GNS truck.

"What's all the fuss about?" she asked Miller, a blank expression on her face. "Anything wrong with our signal?"

Miller adjusted his camera, then looked at Sheila.

"Oh no, the signal will be fine, as soon as we get the body off the mast."

Sheila looked up and shrieked, "My God, it's Cav Campbell!"

Even in the dark, punctuated by the camera lights and the flashing lights on the squad cars, Sheila knew the dead celebrity immediately.

His tan had not yet begun to turn death gray. Sheila had seen Campbell a dozen times with Bren Forrest. Now and then she would see something about him in the local alternate online newspaper, The Riot. Years earlier he was popping up on TMZ or Pop Tarts with some regularity, but not much anymore.

Sheila choked back a gag and looked up at the mast again.

"It's Cav, it's our Cav, it's..."

She swallowed hard, brushed aside a strand of otherwise well-trained hair and turned to Miller.

"Does this mean we'll go live any minute?"

Ten feet away, Cassandra Page heard what Sheila had said. She walked closer and realized that Sheila was right.

She grabbed the phone again. Chuck, pick up dammit, she said to herself as the phone rang back at Channel 3.

"Chuck, Cassie here. We have the story of the year here, Chuckie, so I suggest we break in and go live now or else you're going to be under the viaduct with a sign saying, 'Will produce TV shows for food,' get it?"

Chuck didn't respond but Cassie could hear a lot of loud voices in the newsroom.

"Chuck, Chuck, listen. Cav Campbell, the movie star, Bren Forrest's boy toy, is hanging suspended over the driveway here on the mast of the GNS live truck. His fiancée is upstairs at a party with the mayor, the police chief and every other important person between here and the Antarctic. I'm, what? Call who? Hell, call the Milkman himself if you have to but we need to go live now!"

Inside the GNS live truck, the engineer was on the phone with the writer at GNS headquarters downtown. It was his second call, a few minutes after the first.

"No shit. Sheila says it's Cav Campbell. Yeah, the Cav Campbell, honest to God. What? Did he fall?

"Hell, I don't know if he fell or jumped or what, but he must have been at that party for the boss. Yeah, our boss, Bren Forrest.

"Right. Sheila is here, yeah, yeah. But the dish is off the mast. We'll have to prop it up on the van roof and go with it.

"The picture may not be great, but we can't do… Jesus, no we can't put it back on the mast. There's a body there. Get somebody out here with a LiveU. Meantime, send us what you can see on your monitor with your cell phone. We need help out here!"

He pocketed the phone and hollered out the back of the truck toward Sheila.

"We're going live in five, grab this mic here, and your IFB!"

Sheila ran to the truck and clipped the little microphone onto the lapel of her black linen jacket, pulling a thread as she did. That never happened before.

Sheila was distraught. She had not put on her TV makeup yet and the humidity and heat had made her hair a mess, she just knew it.

"I gotta fix up," she said, as Miller handed her the IFB, the earpiece attached to a wire going to a small transmitter on her belt. It allowed her to hear what went on the air, plus instructions from the producer and director in the control room at GNS headquarters.

IFB is short for "interrupted feedback." Most reporters had more colorful names for it and for the off-air people who liked to shout orders through it at the on-camera talent. To Sheila, however, the IFB was her substitute masters degree.

Her producers knew how little she knew about so much of what she covered. They often made her seem smarter than she was with timely information on the IFB.

Sheila did know, however, that Cav Campbell had died on TV, literally, and that she had a worldwide scoop in the making.

ABOUT THE AUTHORS

Marco Island Writers' Inc.

Motto:
"Writers Helping Writers"

Mission Statement:
To gather writers of all genres and skill levels, to help one
another improve his or her craft by sharing information
and inspiration regarding writing or publishing
for fun or profit.

Robert Dean Bair
1926-2019

Bob was born in 1926, Ohio. He worked as an insurance investigator, industrial engineer, management consultant and served as President of an aeronautical products company. A member of the First Army Special Troops, Bob served at Governor's Island, New York Harbor. He was one of the charter members of Marco Island Writers and extremely proud of that role.

Bob published seven books between 2013 and 2017.
The Rob Royal mystery series:
Rob Royal at Lambeth Bridge
Rob Royal Covert Operations
Peace at Lambeth Bridge
The Director
The Overthrow of Juan Bosch,
The Cloisters of Canterberry
White House and Beyond

All are based on his life experiences.

Dr. Dolores Burton

Dr. Dolores Burton is an award-winning author with many books. As a Fulbright Senior Scholar, she worked nationally and internationally to improve teaching and learning for students of all ages. Her writing reflects her passion for helping all students succeed. The Complete Guide to RtI: An Implementation Toolkit (2011); Mathematics, the Common Core; and RtI: An Integrated Approach to Teaching in Today's Classrooms (2013), contain instructional strategies for teachers and parents. A middle-grade chapter book, A Story of Courage: Supreme Court Justice Sonia Sotomayor, was published in 2017.

Her picture books: But You Don't Look Like Me!; Bully Billy Is Back! The Burrowing Owls Are Worried; Big Bad Barry: Does He Really Want to Be a Bully?; and NEW hard cover But You Don't Look Like Me! A Tale of Kindness and Friendship use owl characters to demonstrate kindness, acceptance of individual differences and research based anti-bullying strategies. All books are available on Amazon.com and her exciting new website, BreaklightPublications.com.

Vince D'Angelo
October 1927 - August 22, 2021

It is difficult to summarize the life and character of Vince, who's experiences encompassed multiple disciplines as real estate developer, entrepreneur, pilot, flight instructor, writer, golfer, meticulous home-maker, eccentric inventor and innovator. He was also a parent, with three children and two grandchildren.

Born October of 1927, Vince grew up in Brooklyn and Eastchester, New York, later attending Columbia University to study architecture. Vince served during the Korean conflict, then enlisted in the Navy where his experiences in the Western Pacific Region became the subject of his written works later in life.

After an early retirement at 62, Vince moved to Naples, Florida. His new life was equally full and impressive. He ran a flight business, trained pilots, aided the Civil Air Patrol, wrote freelance articles in aviation magazines, golfed, and enjoyed his newly discovered love of fiction writing, publishing several, while giving freely of his time and talent to Marco Island Writers.

Vince D'Angelo's Written Works

Out of Hong Kong   Forever is Tomorrow
No-Name Island   Bavarian Girls

Excised with permission, from an obituary written
by his granddaughter, Alexa.
Some of his books are available on Amazon.com

Jean Duling

Jean Saunders Duling, teacher, poet, and artist, opens her soul to the reader in a piece of writing, "It Is Not Your Time", as she shares her near death experience and learns hope, to cope with Multiple Sclerosis (MS) and major changes in her life. Jean, widow, mother of two, and grandmother of three girls was born in Plymouth MA where history came alive. She is a graduate of Keene State College, Keene, New Hampshire and student of Lifetime Learning. She lived in Marco Island, Florida for several years and now in Lyman, Maine most of the year.

Her first book of poetry, Wing Songs is used as a teaching text and her second book of poetry, Winds of Time, she calls her book of recovery after a head injury. After the diagnosis of MS, her booklet Marco Island A-Z came to life. It is a coloring book for all ages.

Don Erdek
December 21, 1935 – August 16, 2020

Don was born on December 21, 1935, in Manville, a small New Jersey factory town where he spent his early childhood. He graduated with high honors from Rutgers University in 1963 earning a degree in chemistry. He took a position with prestigious Bell Labs in Murray Hill, New Jersey and continued his education with a graduate study program in chemical physics at the Brooklyn Institute of Technology. He moved to Miami, Florida in 1965 and shortly thereafter took a job on Eniwetok Atoll in the South Pacific followed by one in Tripoli Libya, then one in Saudi Arabia that lasted some eighteen years more. He retired in May 1991 at the age of fifty-six. He was lured out of retirement to take a position with Johnson Controls at Cape Canaveral. Working at the Cape on the space program and specifically on the launch towers was an exciting challenge. He retired once again in 1996 and purchased a seventy-three-acre ranch in Colmesneil, Texas in the deep East Texas piney woods. Was a rancher for seventeen years on one of the most beautiful pieces of God's green Earth. Moved to Naples, Florida in 2015.

He decided it was time to write a book with a poetic take on life, which led to his first book "Inner Sanctum." Don found he still had many stories and poems he wanted to share so he collected them into his book, "The Ochre Hand." Available on Amazon.com.

Don Farmer
September 27, 1938 – March 31, 2021

As a little boy, Don Farmer wanted to be a foreign correspondent. He began his career as a teenager, reporting for his hometown newspaper in suburban St. Louis, Missouri. At the end of his career, he had been a successful newspaper and radio reporter, a novelist and non-fiction author, national and local TV anchorman, network television political reporter and war correspondent.

Don wrote three books: Roomies, anecdotes from his life as a network correspondent, and two murder thrillers, Deadly News and Fatal Ambition. After his retirement to Marco Island from his career in TV News, he was a radio host, a columnist for local newspapers and a novelist.

Don began his career as a correspondent and bureau chief at home and abroad for ABC News. He covered world and domestic news events as a news anchor for CNN at its inception, working with his wife, Chris Curle. They anchored at the ABC station in Atlanta before their permanent move to Marco.

Don and Chris were part-time or full-time residents of Marco for forty-seven years.

His books are available on Amazon.com.

Don Fedor

Donald (Don) B. Fedor [pen name D.F. Dawson], is Professor Emeritus, Georgia Institute of Technology, Atlanta, GA. He received his Ph.D. in Organizational Behavior from the University of Illinois, Champaign-Urbana. He co-authored the book, Change the Way You Lead Change with David M. Herold (Stanford University Press). Don has training in Theta Healing™, is a longtime member of Edgar Cayce's A.R.E., and is a student of A Course in Miracles. Don lives in Southwest Florida.

Books available on Amazon.com

Daniel Goldstein
1923- 2018

Dan was born in Revere, Massachusetts. When he was a sophomore in high school, he dropped out in order to join the Air Force but later completed his high school diploma and went on to a degree at Northeastern University, Boston.

He and his wife, Rochelle moved to Naples when retired.

Dan published six books between 2012 - 2016
Biography: Wild Bill Hickok
Suspense novels: Destination Croatia
Boston/Moscow Connection
The Romanov Star
Processing the Mafia

Children's book: Dingus Magee

Some of his books are available on Amazon.com

Pauline Hayton

From the northeast of England, Pauline Hayton worked as a probation officer in her hometown of Middlesbrough before immigrating to the United States in 1991 with her husband Peter. Among other things, for many years now Pauline has given generously of her time to both mentor other writers and learn through being a member of Marco Island Writers. She and her husband also sponsor Mount Kisha English School in Magulong, a remote village in Nagaland, India. All the royalties from her books support the school and help the children obtain a second-ary education. She lives in Naples, Florida, a willing slave to four cats who adopted her in the Great Recession. Hayton is the author of nearly a dozen books and/or podcasts, the latest of which can be found on Vella, Molly's Heroes.

https://www.amazon.com/Pauline-Hayton/e/B003YGSLJY

Melody Highman

Melody Highman rediscovered her long-neglected muse while going cross-eyed watching her laundry tumble in a one-chair Uluru laundromat. There, in Australia's dusty Red Center, she plucked a novel from the laundromat's sharing library and inspiration sparked in her brain: That's the kind of novel I want to write! She tracked that author down, mentored with her, and studied the writing craft over the following four years as she and her husband slow traveled the globe, living like locals in more than thirty countries.

When home, she resides in Florida with husband Cliff, also afflicted with wanderlust, and weaves the sights, sounds and tastes of their travel experiences into her writing, evoking a strong sense of place and vivid character development.

Her debut paranormal novel, The Stylist, currently available on Kindle Vella, takes place on England's Channel coast. Also in the works is a cozy mystery series depicting the fun and foibles of an American couple exploring the world as international housesitters.

Melody helps other writers as a professional beta reader and developmental editor. Stay tuned!

Donna Kremer

Donna Kremer has been a lover of writing since having received a diary and a metal tin full of cat stationery on her tenth birthday. Her "commonplace book" of quotes culled from books, radio, movies, and witty friends spans nearly forty years.

She splits her time between a small northern Michigan town, a log cabin with frequent beavers as neighbors, and a high-falutin house in southern Florida that could use a few chickens. This is her first short story.

James Masciarelli

James Masciarelli is a writer, coach, and serial entrepreneur. His leadership roles span social work, high-tech human resources, executive search, board governance, and angel investing. Known for thought leading articles in professional publications, his first book, PowerSkills is considered the seminal book on relationship management for personal, career and business success.

His recent action/adventure novel, Beyond Beauport features a female protagonist on a midlife quest for her seafaring and pirate ancestry. James and creative wife Judi enjoy endless summers in Naples, Florida and Gloucester, Ma. He collects friends and vintage guitars.

Books available on Amazon.com

Michael M. Meguid M.D.

Born in Egypt, Michael Meguid spent his childhood in Germany and England, attending University College Hospital Medical School, London, followed by Surgical Residency at Harvard Medical School. As a surgeon/scientist in Oncology and Clinical Nutrition, he earned a PhD in Nutrition at MIT to benefit cancer patients, and founded and is now Editor Emeritus of, the International Journal, Nutrition. While operating and researching at Upstate Medical University, Syracuse he ran a research laboratory which was funded by the National Institutes of Health for twenty-five years. He and his team authored over 400 scientific papers. His research has won awards and continues to be cited to this day. He is the recipient of numerous national and international honors. On retiring, he earned an MFA from Bennington Writers Seminars, Vermont and attended workshops at Queens University of Charlotte, North Carolina, and Non-fiction Seminars at Goucher College. Maryland. Meguid's short stories have been published in Bennington Review, Stone Canoe, Columbia Medical Review, Hektoen International and the Marco Island Writer's anthologies. He lives and writes on Marco Island, Florida.

Books available on Amazon.com

Nancy Murvine

Nancy Murvine is a published poet, writer, and essayist. While teaching in Delaware, she received a grant as an emerging artist and gave poetry readings and workshops throughout the mid-Atlantic area. She now resides in Florida where she continues to hone her writing and has been recognized with several awards for her short stories from Florida Weekly magazine. She is currently working on a book of short stories and a novel.

Ryszarda (Lida) Pelc

Ryszarda Pelc was a high school teacher in Poland before coming to the United States for the first time in 1985. Her husband Karol had been invited by the Michigan Technological University as a guest professor and invited him to stay. The couple settled down in Houghton, a small town located in the Keweenaw Peninsula, a thin strip of land embraced by Lake Superior in the northern part of Michigan State. She became a part time resident of Marco Island in 1993.

Lida, as she likes friends to call her, joined many clubs, to help her to speak English, then found that writing improved it even better, so she enrolled in several creative writing classes. Writing poetry in her native language, Polish, started only later, after she started to feel comfortable writing in English.

Ms. Pelc writes mostly about nature, like the beauty of snow or the landscape. After traveling to Japan, she started to write Haiku (minimalist poems). In 1989, she published her first collection of poems, entitled Fascination. Her blog, at lidapelc. blogspot.com gives accounts of others, appearing in American Poetry Anthology 1999, Great Poems of the Western World, The Best Poems of 1996, and Songs of Honor. Besides poems, she writes essays, short stories and articles.

Virginia Read

Virginia Colwell Read was born in Auburn, New York, graduated from the University of Virginia's Mary Washington College, moved to Georgetown, D. C, where she briefly taught school in Arlington, VA before going to work for the U. S. Government.

During her years of volunteer work she has written or edited reports and newsletters for many local and national organizations. She served as president of the Friends of the National Symphony Orchestra, Milwaukee Historical Society, Milwaukee Chapter of Archaeological Institute of America; and on the boards of the Milwaukee University School Mothers, the Summerville, S.C. Garden Club, and a Girl Scout and United Way leader for fifteen years. She was a Pioneer founder of the Naples Botanical Garden, a Gunston Hall Regent, and the Colonial Dames of America Co-Chairman of the George Mason Memorial in Washington, D.C.

Virginia has had poems and short stories in Wisconsin and Florida literary magazines and won a number of honorary prizes. She is a member of the Calusa Garden Club, the Native Plant Society, D.A.R. and Marco Island Writers

Dmitriy Shoutov, Ph.D.

In the sixth year after the end of World War Two, I saw the light of life. Under my mother's passionate love, my childhood was the happiest time. Even though I had to follow her traditional teaching of structure and discipline. Hungry for knowledge, I studied German, English, Korean, Chinese, and Japanese, and graduated from Moscow University and the Academy of Foreign Trade. Continued education was received at the Universities in Pyongyang, Nanjing, and Columbia University in New York City. During my long career at the United Nations, I wrote technical reports on how to improve living standards in the developing world. My interest in literary writing came later when I published documentary narrative stories in local newspapers in the United States and Beijing Review (China). Journey to Love is my first effort in poetry, where I contemplate a complex feeling of love. Day by day, we are getting older. Love does not.

Joanne Simon Tailele

Joanne Simon Tailele grew up in the Youngstown, Ohio area, and wrote her first short story at the age of ten. Beginning her commercial writing career in 2010, it took multiple publications before she realized that her brand is mother-daughter stories. As a mother of four, a grandmother of ten and a great-grandmother of one, family is a natural topic. Ms. Tailele has published four Women's Fiction, two biographies and two children's books. She is currently adding to her children's book series, Carly's Island Adventures. Ms. Tailele is also the owner of Simon Publishing LLC, a small independent press catering to the authors that seek a personal touch. www.SimonPublishingLLC. When not writing, editing, or publishing, she dabbles in real estate. She loves spending time on the beaches of the Gulf of Mexico. She lives in Naples, FL. with her beloved husband and two ornery cats.

www.JoanneTailele.com and Amazon.com

Linda Walker

Linda Walker, a member of Marco Island Writers for several years, is NOT a New York Times Best-Selling Author. She has written several plays for the benefit of Red Bird Mission School in which she also acts and directs. Having written both news and human-interest articles for a community newspaper in Ohio, she now proofreads and writes for a local community newsletter. After attending playwriting and poetry writing classes she has found a new outlet for her work by reading her poems and essays on open-mic night.

George Walmsley
1937 - 2017

George was born in Philadelphia. He served in the United States Air Force for four years and flew B-47 bombers. He graduated college with a degree in Law/Justice & Public Administration.

George became a police officer in New Jersey. He retired as Deputy Chief of Police. When he moved to Naples, he was a charter member of the Naples Press Club and a long-time member of MIW.

He was the co-writers with Helvi Walmsley on two articlesfor the S.F. Territorial News.

George published seven books between 2013-2015:
The Virtuoso
The Virtuoso, A Sequel
An Affair to Remember
The Pianoman
Plowshares to Sabers
Through the Looking Glass
Sophia - a Memoir
American Fly-Boy

Most of his books are available on Amazon.com

Jennie Schwartz Weckelman

Jennie, originally a Midwesterner, has also called the Caribbean and England home for several years each, but Florida has been her home since 1994. Some of those years were in Key Largo, but the last twenty-five in Naples. Mother of one, stepmother of four, with formal training in the law & real estate, her keen interest in history and the human condition come together in her writing. She draws material from a deep well of experiences in business ownership, resort management, Brittany Spaniel shows/training, living abroad, and community service.

A member of Marco Island Writers for several years, Jennie has served as Secretary of the organization as well as Editor of the Newsletter, Website, and this anthology. Her volume of work, so far, has been acquired and/or published in Genealogy Digest, Fenton Area Community Guide 1983-1984, and Marco Island Writers Anthology Vol V & VI. She is currently working on a novel, Commander Good, weaving the fictional exploits of an ancestor with real history.

CHARITBLE ORGANIZATIONS

Marco Island Writers believe in giving back to the community. A portion of our proceeds go to support literacy for children here in SW Florida, and abroad at the Mt. Kisha School in India.

www.ingramcontent.com/pod-product-compliance
Lightning Source LLC
Chambersburg PA
CBHW061215210726
48294CB00006B/1848